FROM THE NANCY DREW FILES

ASSIGNMENT: Find a missing rock star—Bent Fender's lead guitarist, Barton Novak, *who disappeared suddenly after telling Nancy he had something important to tell her.*

CONTACT: Roger Gold, *Bent Fender's drummer, whose father is a friend of Carson Drew's.*

SUSPECTS: Ann Nordquist, *the group's agent. She may have decided that ten percent isn't enough. Maybe she's going for it all.*

George Marshall, *the producer of Fender's hit records. Could he also be producing pirate editions of those same tunes?*

Dave Peck, *a friend of Ned Nickerson's, with a mysterious new job, and lots of cash to flash around.*

Alan Wales, *Bess Marvin's new boyfriend, who'd give anything to be a success in the rock world. How far is he willing to go?*

COMPLICATIONS: How do you prove there's been a kidnapping when there's no ransom note? And how do you investigate a case when all the clues lead straight to your best friend's boyfriend? But Nancy has to hang in there. Barton's life is in danger—and before the case is over, so is hers!

THE
NANCY DREW FILES™

Carolyn Keene

GREY CASTLE PRESS

This novel is a work of fiction. Names, characters, places and incidents are either the product of the author's imagination or are used fictitiously. Any resemblance to actual events or locales or persons, living or dead, is entirely coincidental.

First Grey Castle Edition, March 1988

Published in Large Print by arrangement with Simon & Schuster, Inc.

Printed in Canada

Library of Congress Cataloging-in-Publication Data

Keene, Carolyn.
Deadly intent—1st Grey Castle ed.

p. cm.—(The Nancy Drew files)
Summary: Nancy's assignment is to find a missing rock star. Bent Fender's lead guitarist, Barton Novak, who disappeared suddenly after telling Nancy he had something important to tell her.
1. Large type books. [1. Mystery and detective stories. 2. Rock music—Fiction. 3. Large type books.] I. Title. II. Series: Keene, Carolyn. Nancy Drew Files.
PZ7.K23Of 1988 [Fic]—dc19 88-13

ISBN 0-942545-23-0 (lg. print)
ISBN 0-942545-28-1 (lib. bdg. : lg. print)

DEADLY
INTENT

Chapter One

"COME ON, BESS, cool it," Nancy Drew whispered. "People are starting to stare."

But Bess Marvin seemed not to hear her best friend's voice. "I just can't believe it!" she gushed. "It's all too much! New York City, Radio City Music Hall, the Bent Fender concert . . ."

"The hottest rock band around," said Alan Wales, Bess's latest boyfriend. "And they've invited us backstage!"

"Oh, George, help me with these star-struck kids," teased Nancy. "I think your cousin has gone off the deep end."

"Well, you have to admit, this *is* going to be

one incredible vacation," George Fayne said, falling in step with the group.

"The best," Nancy declared, running a hand through her reddish-blond hair. "And no mysteries, just fun. This detective needs a little break."

At eighteen, Nancy had already earned a reputation as one of the nation's top young detectives, solving mysteries all across the country, and overseas as well. Her most recent one, though, *Secrets Can Kill,* had started in a high school just a few miles from her hometown of River Heights.

"Well, maybe you need a break, Nan, but *I* can think of one mystery I wouldn't mind solving," Bess spoke up.

George threw her cousin a puzzled look. "Since when are you into detective work?"

Nancy was puzzled, too. George was always eager to jump right in and help her on a case, no matter how dangerous, but Bess usually had to be coaxed. Unraveling mysteries scared her, and she was the first to admit it.

"Yeah, what mystery do you want to solve?" Nancy asked.

Bess giggled. "The mystery in Barton Novak's big green eyes," she answered. "I wonder if he's as gorgeous in real life as he is on MTV."

"I should have figured." George let out an exasperated sigh. "You're not planning on doing anything to embarrass us in front of him and the rest of the band, are you?"

"Yeah, don't go getting any ideas," joked Alan, pulling Bess closer to him.

"Hey, guys, don't worry. One guitarist is enough for me." Bess stood on tiptoe and gave Alan a kiss.

In the few weeks since they'd met, Bess and Alan had been inseparable—joined at the lip, Nancy liked to joke. They reminded her of the way things used to be between her and Ned Nickerson.

Nancy found herself wishing for those days. But then, it had been her own choice to get involved with Daryl Gray during her last mystery. And although it was over with him almost before it started, she couldn't blame Ned for feeling miffed. Since then, she had visited Ned once at Emerson College, and he had come to River Heights for a weekend, but things had been cooler than usual between them, and that hurt. She could only hope they could put the past behind them.

"Nancy Drew! Earth to Nancy!" Bess tapped the top of Nancy's head. "Anyone home up there?"

"Sorry, Bess. What—?"

"I said that of course Alan's my number one guitarist, but it *is* pretty incredible that we're going to meet Barton Novak in a few seconds, isn't it?"

Returning to the exhilaration of the moment, Nancy smiled. She remembered the thrill she'd felt listening to Bent Fender and how she'd followed their rise from struggling performers to top stars.

Alan echoed Bess's enthusiasm. "I've memorized practically every song Barton's ever recorded. The first thing I ever figured out how to play on my own was the lead for 'Break Down the Walls.'" He moved his hands, playing imaginary notes on an air guitar. "I'm so psyched that you guys are taking me along tonight!"

"Alan, how could we not take our favorite future rock star to meet our favorite current rock star?" Nancy smiled and gave him a light punch on the arm. "Besides, Dad said the musicians in the band were happy to have us all."

Nancy's father, a lawyer, was negotiating the band's new recording agreement. Normally, Carson Drew worked on criminal cases. But Bent Fender's drummer, Roger Gold, was the son of his old college roommate, Sy Gold, who had recently moved to a town not far from River Heights. He and Nancy's father had rekindled their old friendship, and now Carson Drew was doing Mr. Gold a favor by working on the contract for his son's band. In return, Roger and the band were letting Nancy and her friends come backstage for one of their concerts, and they were going to give them a personal guided tour of the New York rock clubs.

"What a mob scene," Nancy said as she and

her friends edged through the crowd of noisy fans in front of the Music Hall. Off on one side of the building, Nancy caught sight of a polished brass door.

"This is it, the stage door!" she exclaimed, mounting a few steps and pushing the door open. Just inside, in a glass booth, sat two burly security guards in identical tan uniforms.

"Hi," Nancy said. "Roger Gold told us to come back and see him before the show."

The bearded guard frowned wearily. "Young lady, do you know how many times we've heard that one?"

"But it's true," Nancy insisted. "His father is a friend of my father's. He's expecting us."

The guards exchanged glances. "Why don't you kids give us a break?" the other one said. "There have been at least a dozen folks in here already, trying to get to see the band. We—"

"Roger said you'd page him when we arrived," Nancy interrupted, remaining polite.

The guards exchanged another glance.

"Listen," Nancy persisted, "I'll make you a deal. You let Roger know Nancy Drew and her friends are here, and if he doesn't want to see us, we'll leave. I promise."

The guard with the beard shrugged and picked up the telephone.

"Way to go, Nan," whispered George.

A few seconds later, the guard was hanging up the receiver, an apologetic look on his face. "I really thought—I mean, so many kids come back here—"

"No problem," Nancy said. "You were just doing your job."

"He said he'll meet you downstairs."

The guard pointed to the elevators. "Jeez." He scratched his head. "I could have sworn you were just another bunch of crazy fans."

"We are," Alan called back as they headed for the elevators. "But we're a lucky bunch of crazy fans!"

Nancy laughed. Alan had hit the nail on the head. From the moment she'd heard Bent Fender's first single, she'd been hooked. And now she was about to get a behind-the-scenes look at one of their concerts. It wasn't just any concert, either. It was the first of Fender's 'Rock for Relief' shows, a series of benefits to aid handicapped children.

A wave of excitement washed over Nancy as she and her friends got into the elevator. She smoothed her hand over her short, electric blue skirt and picked a thread off her oversized sweater. Her long, lean legs were flattered by a pair of patterned tights, which looked perfect with her favorite ankle boots.

"Don't worry. You look great, as usual," Bess told her. "You too, George," she added, eyeing George in the simple black jumpsuit that hugged every line of her athletic body. "Boy, what I would give to be able to wear an outfit like that."

"You look pretty fabulous yourself," George returned. "I love that turquoise shirt with your blond hair."

"You don't think it makes me look too fat?"

"No way," Alan said. "You look perfect." He was wearing tight jeans and a T-shirt, the picture of a rock-and-roller. Bess reached up to tie a turquoise bandanna around his neck.

"Same color as your shirt," George grinned. "Looks like you're color-coding your boyfriend."

The elevator door slid open, and the friends stepped out. There, looking just as Nancy had pictured him, stood Roger Gold, unmistakable with his spiky black hair and single silver earring.

"Hi," he said easily.

There was an uncomfortable silence as Nancy and her friends studied the legend standing before them.

Roger smiled at each of them in turn, his gaze finally coming to rest on Alan. "Well, *you're* not Nancy," he joked.

Nancy took a step forward. "No, I am," she said, not quite believing that she was talking to a superstar like Roger Gold. "And these are Bess and George and Alan." She indicated each of her friends in turn.

"Hello," they chorused nervously. Nancy saw how tongue-tied they looked.

"Nice to meet you all," Roger responded. Then he said, "Nancy, I've been hearing stories about your father ever since I can remember. My dad claims they were the best roommate team in the history of college life."

"Yeah, my dad says the same thing." Nancy was still a bit awed by Roger's presence. Although Barton Novak's name was almost synonymous with Bent Fender, Nancy had always felt most loyal to Roger. After all, their fathers had been best buddies. Nancy had not met Roger before, since he had grown up with his mother outside of Los Angeles, but she'd known about him long before he'd become a star.

"Did your dad ever tell you about the time he and my dad got into the kitchen at the dining hall—" Roger began.

"—and colored the mashed potatoes purple," finished Nancy. She laughed, loosening up. Roger was so open and friendly that he made it easy to remember that stars were people too. "And how about when they had that ten-foot-long submarine sandwich delivered to their history class?"

"Yeah. That's one of my dad's favorite stories," Roger said. "So where is your father, anyway?"

"Back at the hotel, getting ready for the opera. He's not too big on what he calls 'that music you kids listen to.'" She gave an embarrassed shrug.

"Hey, don't worry about it. Your dad told

Barton and me that he wasn't into rock when we talked to him about our contract. To each his own." Roger hesitated. "Hey, listen, let me introduce you to the rest of the band. They're in the lounge having a little preshow Ping-Pong match. Linda's our resident champ. She's wasting Barton."

Nancy saw George's face light up at the mention of Linda Ferrare, Bent Fender's bass player and backup vocalist. George was a great fan of Linda's tough, powerful voice and dynamic style.

Roger led them to the lounge and pushed open the door. There, at one end of the Ping-Pong table in the center of the room, stood Barton Novak, his brow creased in concentration beneath a shock of blond hair. Bess let out an audible sigh. Barton snapped his paddle as the ball came toward him. On the other side of the table, Linda prepared to return the shot. She slammed the ball so hard it went speeding out at a crazy angle, bouncing at the very corner of Barton's side of the table. He took a wild swing and missed.

"Game," said Linda, tossing her curly dark hair.

There was a smattering of applause from the rest of the band members. Mark Bailey, the other guitarist, was sitting in an armchair; Jim Parker, the keyboard player, was on the couch.

"Nice shot." Barton wiped his forehead. Then he looked toward the door for the first time. His expression lightened up. "Hey, gang, we've got guests. Hiya."

"Guys," Roger said, "this is Nancy Drew. I was telling you about her. And these are her friends, Bess, Alan, and Georgia."

"George," she corrected.

"Sorry." Roger grinned. "So, all of you, say hello to Mark, Jim, Linda, and Barton." Roger pointed to each person, but Nancy had studied Fender's album covers enough to know the band members instantly.

"Thanks for inviting us to come tonight," Nancy said to them.

"The pleasure's ours," Barton replied gallantly. "We get to have the hottest detective around at our show tonight."

Nancy could feel heat rising to her cheeks. Barton's face had been on the cover of *Rolling Stone, Time, People,* and half a dozen other major magazines, and he was complimenting *her.* "I am beginning to make a name for myself," she said humbly.

"Beginning? From what I hear, you've done it." He looked at Nancy. "If you don't mind, I'd like to talk to you after we're finished playing tonight." Nancy cocked her head. Did she detect a note of urgency in Barton's voice?

"I'd be glad to," she said, trying to read his expression. But if he was worried about something, he gave no further clue. Instead he joined in the enthusiasm of her friends.

"This is a dream come true for me," Alan blurted. "I'm Fender's biggest fan. And I've learned a lot by listening to you," he said to Barton.

"You play guitar?"

Alan nodded. "I mean, I'm no—well, no Barton Novak." He grinned. "But I'm getting better all the time."

"Do you play in a band?" Jim Parker wanted to know.

"The Mud Castles," Alan answered. "We've been getting gigs in some clubs and bars around River Heights."

"The Mud Castles?" Roger turned to Alan and studied his face closely. "Hey, you know, I think I heard you when I was visiting my old man a few months ago. Did you play a bar over in the South End—Puffy's or Puffer's or something?"

"Puffin's. Yeah, that was us. But how come we didn't recognize you?"

"I had on dark glasses and a hat," Roger said, almost apologetically. "It's nice to be able to go out like a regular guy once in a while, have a couple of beers. But I had to leave when someone at a table near the bar started giving me funny looks. I just didn't want to hassle with anyone figuring out who I was."

Nancy tried to picture Roger in her hometown bar, rubbing elbows with people she'd known all her life.

"Yeah, I like that little place," he went on.

"And Alan, your band was terrific. You play lead, right?"

Alan nodded.

Roger turned to his fellow band members. "This kid is okay." He jabbed his finger in Alan's direction. "More than okay. Someday he'll put us out of business if we're not careful!"

The smile on Alan's face could have lit up the entire room. Nancy flashed Bess a thumbs-up sign.

"We'll be out of business sooner than you think," Linda interjected, "if we're not on stage in half an hour." She looked at Nancy and the others. "Make yourselves comfortable. Play some Ping-Pong or something while we get ready."

"We'll be back soon," Barton Novak broke in, "and then we'll take you out to the wings to watch the show."

Nancy grinned. She sensed that this night—this rock concert—would be special.

George was going for the game point twenty minutes later when the lounge door burst open. The ball flew by unheeded as Roger Gold appeared in the doorway.

"Show time?" Nancy asked excitedly, putting down her Ping-Pong paddle. Then she saw the worried expression on Roger's face as his eyes darted around the room.

"Barton's not here?" Roger was trying to

sound calm, but Nancy could hear the edge of panic in his voice. His hands were clenched, knuckles white, on the doorframe.

"What's wrong, Roger?" she asked.

"Barton's disappeared. I've looked all over the building, and he's gone."

"Disappeared?" George finally caught the bouncing Ping-Pong ball. "Maybe he just went out to get some air."

"Five minutes before we go on? No way!" Roger took a deep breath. "I've got a bad feeling about this. Real bad."

Chapter Two

NANCY STOOD IN Barton's dressing room with her friends and the rest of Bent Fender. On the vanity lay uncapped tubes and containers of stage makeup. An open can of Cherry Coke was almost full. A guitar was leaned up in the corner of the room, next to a portable amplifier.

"It looks like he was right in the middle of getting ready," Nancy said. "Not like he planned on going anywhere."

"You're sure?" Roger asked.

"There's no question about it," Nancy replied grimly, bending down to look under the vanity. A pair of cowboy boots—the ones the rock star always wore on stage—sat on the floor.

"Barton had these on when we were introduced to him before. That means—"

"—that wherever he is, he's barefoot," George finished.

"Exactly. That's why I don't think he intended to leave this room."

"You mean he was just sitting here, and then . . ." Bess's voice trailed off.

"*Something* happened. Maybe someone knocked on his door and he got up to answer it." Nancy thought out loud, trying to piece the puzzle together. She felt herself switching gears, the excitement she'd experienced at meeting her rock idols melting into the clear, quick thinking that had earned her her reputation as a detective.

She pulled open the door to the little dressing room, just as Barton might have done. Across the corridor was a rehearsal studio for the Rockettes, who danced in special shows at Radio City Music Hall. Lights from the street washed through the room, glinting off the mirrors lining one wall. The hallway between the two rooms was littered with stage props and lighting equipment.

Nancy stepped out of the room to inspect the jumble of boxes, painted scenery, and other theater paraphernalia. "Hey, you guys, come look at this." A few yards down the hall, the contents of a box of lighting gels was scattered every which way. A papier-mâché tree trunk nearby was broken in half. "Looks like a scuffle," Nancy noted.

"Here's something else," Bess observed. A broken lamp lay on the floor down the hall.

"Wow! There's a whole trail of things!" Nancy said.

"I don't know, Nancy," Linda Ferrare spoke up. "We've performed in a lot of places, and it's not that unusual for the backstage or storage areas to be a jumble of stuff like this." She paused, and her voice dropped. "Besides, I think there's something you ought to know. It's been kept quiet because we don't want the press to find out. But this isn't the first time."

"I don't understand." Nancy surveyed the trail of clues. "Has Barton vanished before?"

"Not exactly." Mark Bailey spoke up. "A few years back—twice—he just took off. We were scared stiff at first because he didn't tell anyone anything, but both times it turned out that he just couldn't cope with the pressure of being a super-celebrity. The first time he flew off to some island in the Mediterranean and rented himself a house on the beach for a few weeks. The second time he spent the weekend with some friends in the country."

"Yeah, but Mark, don't forget, that was two years ago," Roger said, "when we were just starting to make it big. Barton's gotten much better about dealing with his fame." A worried look crossed his face. "I just don't have the same feeling about this."

"Why not?"

"Look," Roger said, "this whole 'Rock for Relief' thing was his idea. I know he's pretty quiet about his sister, but he's totally devoted to her. You know that. He wouldn't let her—or anyone like her—down."

"What does his sister have to do with it?" Nancy asked.

"She's been in a wheelchair all her life," Roger explained. "That's one of the reasons Barton got the idea for these shows. I'm positive that he wouldn't run out on us now. Besides, if he were planning on going, he wouldn't have left all that stuff in his dressing room. Even his guitar is there."

Jim Parker ran a nervous hand through his short dark hair. "But he's got two other guitars, Roger. I don't know. Barton's done some crazy things."

Nancy listened carefully. Barton was beginning to be a real human being to her, with fears and weaknesses like any person. If he had chosen to vanish before, she had to consider the possibility that he might do it again. On the other hand, there was evidence to the contrary.

Nancy sighed. "I can't begin to make guesses about someone I've just met, but I'm inclined to agree with Roger. Vanishing just before a big show like this doesn't make sense and isn't going to be overlooked by the press. If Barton wanted to get away from it all, he couldn't have picked a worse moment to do it."

"Look, everything you're saying sounds reasonable," Linda volunteered, "and it's true that Barton's become more comfortable being, well, being a hot item, but just recently he's been a lot more like the old Barton. I don't know, he seems really uptight about something."

Nancy couldn't help thinking about the urgency she'd sensed when Barton had asked about her detective work. "Linda, do you have any idea what was bothering him?"

Linda shrugged. "Beats me. But he's been acting weird for the past couple of weeks. Ever since . . ."

"Ever since what?"

"Ever since we started talking about our new contract." Linda's olive complexion went pale. She glanced from one member of Bent Fender to the next. "You don't think he's going to leave the band, do you?"

"No way, Lin," Roger reassured her. "Look at the way he's been going at the songs he's writing for the new album. He's totally into the music we're making now." Roger paused. "But he has been tense about the contract." He turned to Nancy to explain. "He thinks we're not getting all the royalties we're entitled to. He started fighting with our agent and our producer. That's why we called your father. We decided to bring in a lawyer."

Nancy nodded. But before she could ask more questions, the telephone in Barton's dressing room rang shrilly.

Mark grabbed the receiver. "Yes?" Pause. "Hey, thanks for calling. Have you found him yet?" His expression darkened, and Nancy held her breath. "Right. Okay, I understand."

"That was the stage manager," Mark said when he hung up. "No trace of Barton, and the audience is getting pretty rowdy. They want to know why we're not on stage. What do we do?"

Jim shook his head thoughtfully. "Whew. All those handicapped kids are out there. We can't let them down."

"Yeah, but how are we supposed to play without the main attraction?" Linda asked, her tough tone barely hiding the concern in her voice. "Boy, if this is Barton's fault, I'm going to make him disappear for good."

"I could cover the leads," Mark said, "but can you imagine doing 'Fever' with one guitar?"

" 'Fever?' What a great tune. I can play every riff in that song," Alan said.

Roger spun around and looked him squarely in the eye.

"Hey, I'm sorry." Alan looked at the ground, embarrassed. "At a time like this I guess no one wants to hear me go on about playing your music."

"No, maybe we do," Roger said, studying Alan intently. "Can you play all our tunes?"

"Well, yeah."

"Really well," Bess added proudly. "He has a great voice, too."

Roger grabbed Barton's guitar from the corner of the room and fiddled with the knobs and dials on the amp. "Try the fast middle section on 'Fever.'" He pressed the guitar into Alan's hands.

Astonishment filled Alan's brown eyes. Roger flashed him a smile of encouragement. "Go ahead," he said.

Nancy listened as Alan tuned the guitar strings and, after taking a long, deep breath, sang the familiar Fender music in a clear, confident voice.

"Not bad." Linda's face was serious, her eyes appraising. "What else can you do?"

"How about 'Little Brother'?" Jim asked, as Alan finished up on 'Fever.' "Do you know that one?"

Alan's brow crinkled in concentration. "That's an oldie," he said, "but I think I can do it." Once again, music filled the room as Alan broke into a slow, dreamy number from Bent Fender's first album.

"What do you say?" Roger addressed his fellow band members. One by one, Nancy saw them signal their approval.

"Champ," Roger said, putting his hand on

Alan's shoulder, "how would you like to be our pinch hitter tonight?"

As if in a fog, Alan put down the guitar. "Me? You want *me* to play with Bent Fender? *Here?*"

"We need your help," Roger said.

"We'll pull you through the rough spots," Mark promised.

Nancy watched as Alan's angular features reflected a rainbow of emotions from doubt to dazed happiness. Then the smile left his face. "What about Barton?" he asked suddenly. "Are you going to call the police?"

"They wouldn't take this seriously," Roger replied gloomily. "Not after the other two times. Barton's earned himself quite a reputation."

"But you can't just do nothing," George said.

Nancy cleared her throat. Despite seeing her dreams of vacation vanishing as rapidly as Barton had, she said, "Look, maybe I could—"

"Nancy, *would* you?" Roger didn't even wait for her to finish her sentence. "I can't tell you how grateful I'd be."

Linda, Jim, and Mark echoed his sentiments.

"Nancy Drew can't turn down a chance to do some sleuthing," George said. "It's in her blood to track down clues."

Nancy had to admit that George was right. Nothing was more of a challenge than solving a mystery. But just then, the tingle of enthusiasm that she usually felt at the beginning of a case was overshadowed by her worries about Barton. Maybe he *was* running away again, but if not, she couldn't lose any time. He might be in terrible danger.

As she combed the halls of the renowned Radio City Music Hall, Nancy could hear strains of the concert coming from the direction of the stage. Alan's playing wasn't as slick or polished as Barton's, but from what Nancy could hear, his fingers were really flying over Barton's guitar. The rest of the band was helping Alan out by covering more of the leads themselves and taking more solos. Still, Alan was winging it like a true pro.

Nancy wished she could be in the wings watching, but finding Barton came first. Bess and George had offered to help her, but she insisted they enjoy the show, telling them she would come get them if she needed their help. Bess, in particular, had looked relieved, obviously not wanting to miss a single note of Alan's performance.

The sounds of the concert grew clearer as Nancy entered an elevator, pressing the button for the street level. When the elevator door slid open and she headed for the guards' booth, the music grew faint again.

The guards and some of Fender's roadies were playing cards. But the bearded guard she had met before looked up from his hand when Nancy asked about Barton. "Novak hasn't shown yet," he said.

"And you haven't seen anyone back here besides the people with the band?"

"The only folks I let in—besides you and your friends—were these guys here," he pointed to the three card-playing roadies, "the gal running the lights, the guy at the sound board, the stage manager, and the two who were unloading equipment before the show."

"What two?" One of the roadies, a lanky, fair-haired young man, put down a can of beer and shot the guard a puzzled look. "We unloaded all the equipment this morning."

The guard frowned. "You're off the wall," he snapped. "Those guys had passes, and they were carrying boxes and stuff."

"They weren't with *us,*" another roadie declared.

Nancy drew in her breath. "Sounds like trouble." She opened her shoulder bag and took out a felt-tipped pen and the tiny notebook she always carried with her. "Tell me everything you can remember about those guys," she said.

"One of 'em was real big—tall with brown hair," said the bearded guard. "How was I supposed to know they didn't belong here? And those boxes—they looked like they had instruments in them, you know—"

"Guitar cases?"

"Yeah, I guess. And they had a huge brown

box, too, looked like the kind that refrigerators are packed in. Actually, they left with that one. Said they were taking out a broken speaker."

Nancy's heart sank, a terrible thought occurring to her. "Was that box large enough to hold a person?"

"I don't believe it!" exclaimed the blond-haired roadie, throwing down his cards. "Did you let some thugs carry Barton out of here in a box, you morons?"

"Please!" Nancy shouted. She got the group calmed down and continued to pump the guards for information about the two unknown men. "Was the tall man's hair straight?" she prodded. "Curly?"

"Straight. Not too much of it, I don't think. I sort of remember a bald spot. And he was a heavy fellow. Dressed in jeans and a jeans jacket."

"What about the other one?" Nancy said.

"Younger. Your age, maybe. Shorter, but he looked strong. Dark wavy hair. Longish. Parted on the side. He had on slacks."

"Gray ones, I think," put in the other guard. "And a button-down shirt. Oh, and he had on a heavy gold chain and a gold ring. I noticed the ring when he showed us their passes. Real different looking, like a sea serpent or something, and it had little red jewels for eyes."

"That's terrific," Nancy said. "Thank you.

Anything else you can think of that might help me?"

"Well," one of the guards said slowly, "we *have* had a little trouble around here lately—break-ins, equipment missing, that sort of thing. But I don't see what that would have to do with Barton."

"All right," said Nancy. "Well, you've been a big help."

"Now what are you going to do?" the roadie asked.

"I want to take one more look around and make sure I didn't miss anything."

Nancy didn't discover anything more in the basement or on the street level. The rehearsal studios were dead ends. But as she poked around near Barton's dressing room, she spotted two black instrument cases. She'd seen the cases earlier and thought nothing of them, but because of her talk with the security guards, she raced over and unlatched them. Empty. They'd probably been carried in just so the two mysterious men would look as if they belonged backstage.

Nancy poked at one of them. It moved slightly, and she noticed something new—a fat wallet. She picked it up, turning it over in her hand. The wallet was made of soft, top-quality leather, decorated on one side with a tooled design of a dragon, its tail curled into the letter L. It was bulging with money.

Nancy ran her finger over the raised leather. Suddenly she remembered the guard's description of the gold ring one man was wearing. He had said it was shaped like a sea serpent—but couldn't the sea serpent have been a dragon?

Eagerly, Nancy opened the wallet to see what other clues she could find, but just as she did she heard a noise behind her. She whipped around and felt a dull thud on her head. It was the last thing she remembered before everything went black.

Chapter Three

THE BACK OF Nancy's head ached when she woke up. Her fingers discovered a large bump, and she rubbed at the soreness. It was then that she recalled being struck. She blinked hard, pulling herself to her feet. The walls around her seemed to spin, and she put her hand out to steady herself.

From the direction of the concert hall came the sound of applause, stamping feet, and cheering fans. Was the show already over? That would mean she'd been out for at least an hour. Taking a few deep breaths, she tried to clear her head. Then she remembered the wallet.

She looked on the floor, under the instrument

cases, behind pieces of scenery, inside boxes of props. The wallet was gone. "What on earth is going on?" she whispered in frustration.

"Nan? Did you say something?" George appeared around the corner, followed by Bess, Alan, and the members of Bent Fender.

"Did you find out anything about Barton?" Roger called to her.

"Did you hear Alan? Wasn't he incredible?" That was Bess.

"Did you miss the whole concert, Nancy?" asked Linda.

"Hey, one person at a time," Nancy replied weakly. Her friends' faces looked blurry.

"Nancy, are you okay? Is something the matter?" George asked. She and Bess rushed to Nancy's side.

"I'm not sure. I found something—that much I know. A wallet. But just as I was taking a look at it, someone hit me over the head, and I blacked out. When I came to, the wallet was gone."

"Someone knocked you out?" Bess's voice was a frightened whisper. "Do you know who did it?"

Nancy shook her head. "Maybe the same people who have Barton. Or maybe just some creep who wanted the wallet. It was full of money, and the guard said there have been some break-ins recently."

"But you said somebody might have taken Barton." Roger Gold's voice trembled.

"Well, I think so. Two men were back here before the show . . ." Nancy told them everything she had found out. "I want to look around a little more," she said, finishing up. "Maybe that wallet wasn't the only thing around that might tell us something. *Ouch.*" She put her hand to her aching head.

"You're not looking for another thing tonight," George told her firmly. "You've got some bump there. We're putting you right to bed and getting you an ice pack."

"But George . . ."

"Your friends are right," Linda said. "In fact, it might be a good idea to have a doctor take a look at you."

"I'm all right, really," Nancy insisted, but as she spoke, the hall began to spin and she felt her knees weaken. She reached out to lean on Bess's shoulder.

"Nancy, the doctor is a good idea," Bess said. "But if there are other clues . . ."

Roger spoke up. "We'll have the security guards search every inch of this place and report back to you if they find anything out of the ordinary."

"Well, okay," Nancy agreed grudgingly. She did feel awfully woozy.

She let the band members put her and her

friends in a taxi to the hotel, but not before promising them that she would be back on the case first thing in the morning.

At the hotel, the house physician gave Nancy a clean bill of health, much to everyone's relief.

Carson Drew had arrived home from the opera to find his daughter in bed in the luxurious suite they were sharing. An ice pack rested on her head, and Dr. Harris was bending over her.

"Dad, you should be getting used to my misadventures by now," Nancy joked weakly.

But the tight lines around Carson Drew's mouth did not soften even after the doctor announced that his daughter was going to be as good as new in the morning. Nancy knew that her father worried about her.

"You go right to sleep and get a solid night's rest," Dr. Harris told Nancy. "That's my prescription."

Nancy nodded sleepily. Once she was alone—her friends in their own suite, her father in the next room—she tried to go over the evening's events in her mind. But she was thoroughly exhausted. Try as she might to stay awake for just a few minutes longer, she felt herself drifting into a deep, dreamless sleep.

"Sleeping beauty," Bess giggled.

"Shh. You'll wake her up," George whispered. "Let's just leave the tray."

"But the omelet will get cold," Bess protested.

"Bess, you know Dr. Harris said she needs rest."

Nancy rolled over and pulled at the quilt that covered her. She opened one eye. Her friends were setting a breakfast tray on the table in the corner of the room. "S'all right, you guys," she mumbled, still half asleep. "I'm getting up."

"Nan! Good morning, sleepyhead." Bess flounced down on the edge of the bed. "How are you feeling?"

Nancy pulled herself into a sitting position, leaning against the backboard of the king-size bed. She checked the bump on her head and found that the swelling had gone down. "Pretty good." She looked around the hotel room. "Hey, it's nice in here, huh?" She hadn't had a chance to look around much when they'd checked in, and after the concert nothing could have been farther from her mind than the hotel room.

"Yeah, and get a load of the view," George said, pulling open the curtains to reveal the skyline of New York's midtown, sparkling in the early-autumn morning sunshine.

"The Empire State Building!" Nancy noted enthusiastically.

"And that other one is the Chrysler Building," Bess informed her. "One of the bellhops told us all about it. Boy, you should have seen him. He was really cute!"

"Bess, honestly," Nancy kidded. "I thought Alan was enough for you."

"Well, I only noticed 'cause I thought maybe George—"

"Thank you very much, cousin dear, but I think I can take care of myself," George interrupted her.

"You guys . . ." Nancy laughed. "Hey, what's on the tray? I'm starved. Whoever gave me that smack on the head did me out of an after-the-show supper."

"Nancy, that's not funny," George said. "You could have really been hurt."

"George, I'm fine. If you should worry about anyone, it's Barton Novak." Nancy grew serious. "Speaking of whom, is there anything new on him?"

George held up a newspaper. Four-inch headlines were splashed all over the front page. Nancy could read them from across the room. ROCK STAR VANISHES, the headlines screamed. "That's the latest," George said. "He still hasn't turned up, and nobody's heard from him."

Nancy pushed off the covers and jumped out of bed. "Time to do some investigating."

"Wait," George protested. "Aren't you even going to have breakfast? We brought it up here for you, and you said you were starved."

"This is more important."

"Nan, I really think you should eat something. You can't miss meals if you're going to start running around the way you do on cases." She brought the breakfast tray to Nancy's night table.

Bess looked longingly at the scalloped potatoes and cheese omelet. "I wish I could put away a breakfast like that and not gain any weight," she said. "You don't know how lucky you are, Nancy."

Nancy sat back down on the bed and took a big bite of a croissant. "All right. You two win." She ate quickly, not tasting much, wanting to get to work as soon as possible. "By the way, where's my dad?"

"He went out jogging. The woman at the front desk told him about a trail in Central Park. He looked in on you before he left, but you were sound asleep. He told us to keep an eye on you." George joined Bess at the edge of Nancy's bed.

"Oh." Nancy wolfed down a few bites of omelet. "I was hoping he could take me over to meet Bent Fender's agent. I know he was planning to see her about their contract this morning."

"Well, he ought to be back soon," Bess said. "But what do you want to talk to that agent for? You think she knows something about Barton?"

"Roger said Barton was fighting with her about their royalties. And with their producer, too. I think that's where I have to start." Nancy took a last swig of orange juice and pushed her tray away.

"Finished?" asked Bess, helping herself to the remaining half a croissant and the last few bites of the potatoes.

At that moment, the door to the hotel suite opened, and Carson Drew stepped in, wearing a navy blue jogging suit and running shoes, his salt-and-pepper hair pushed away from his face with a sweat band.

"Hi, Dad. Did you have a good run?"

"Very nice. Lots of company. I think half the city must be out jogging in the park this morning. How are *you?*" he asked, planting a sweaty kiss on Nancy's forehead.

"Raring to go." Nancy got out of bed and opened her suitcase, taking out her favorite black jeans and a hot pink oversized shirt. "In fact, I wondered if you would mind bringing me with you to Bent Fender's agent this morning. I'm hoping she might be able to give me some information about Barton. Did you see the headlines about him?" She held the newspaper out for her father to look at.

Carson Drew nodded. "I read the article. The media really have a field day when something happens to a big star. They didn't have anything substantial to report, though. Well, perhaps Ann Nordquist can help. I'm meeting her—" Carson Drew checked his watch, "—in forty-five minutes," he said as he headed for his room.

Nancy showered and got dressed quickly. "Do you guys want to meet me for lunch later?" she asked Bess and George. She was whisking on a light dusting of blush and pulling a brush through her hair.

"Sounds good," George said. "How about you, Bess?"

"Can't." Bess shook her head. "I told Alan I'd meet him at the record producers'. Then we'll go out for lunch, just the two of us."

"The same producers who handle Fender?" Nancy shot Bess a quizzical look.

"Yeah. Alan's gone to talk to them about getting a recording contract." Bess was almost exploding with joy. "Nancy," she said, "I know you didn't get to hear him last night. He was incredible! This is the start of something really big. I can just picture screaming fans all around, begging for Alan's autograph, trying to get a glimpse of him, to see him smile—and he'll wade through the crowd and climb into the limousine that's waiting for him." Bess smiled impishly. "Of course, I'll be in the back seat." Bess opened up the locket she always wore around her neck and studied Alan's photograph.

"Don't you think you might be getting the teensiest bit carried away?" Nancy asked gently, trying to avoid jolting Bess out of her fantasy. "I know Alan's got a lot of talent, but only the biggest groups record on the World label. They don't go with unknowns."

"Nan, after last night, Alan is *not* an unknown. They even mentioned him in that newspaper article."

"Okay, Bess, but don't be disappointed if they don't sign him right up. Remember, last night was his first major show, and his job was really to imitate Barton's playing as closely as possible."

"I'm not worried."

George caught Nancy's glance and arched a troubled eyebrow.

"Ready, Nancy?" Carson Drew called.

"Ready," Nancy replied distractedly, her mind on Bess and Alan. She slung her bag over her shoulder. "See you guys," she said, taking one last worried look at her friend as she left. When, she wondered, would Bess's bubble burst?

Chapter Four

NANCY AND HER father entered the twenty-third-floor office of Ann Nordquist's agency. The walls were papered with posters of foreign places.

"I love to travel," Ms. Nordquist explained, after Carson Drew had introduced her to Nancy and explained that Nancy wanted to speak to her for a few minutes. She ran a perfectly manicured hand through her pale blond hair. "I just got back from a tour of mainland China. And the first thing that happens is—that." Ann Nordquist gestured to the day's newspaper Nancy had brought along. "It's awful, isn't it?"

"Yes, it is," replied Nancy. "In fact, that's why I'm here. Ms. Nordquist, Roger Gold told me that you and Barton had been, well, quite frankly, having some problems working together. Something about royalty money."

A tiny frown appeared on Ann Nordquist's forehead. "I wouldn't exactly say we were having problems. You have to understand that royalty revenue is a complicated business. It goes through many channels and often takes some time before it ends up in the artist's pocket. I don't think Barton quite understood that. He felt he was getting shortchanged."

"And he wasn't?"

"I don't think so, not unless something irregular is going on at World."

"They're my next stop," Nancy said. "Maybe you could tell me the names of the people there who handle Barton and Bent Fender."

"Certainly. In fact, I'll make a list for you." The agent reached for a piece of paper, and Nancy studied the attractive woman as she wrote. She had a pleasant, straightforward manner, and she seemed open enough. But Nancy wondered whether there was more to her disagreement with Barton than she'd let on.

"Here you are." Ann Nordquist pushed the list toward Nancy, a half-dozen names written out in her neat, round handwriting. "I ought to warn you about Harold Marshall. He's not the easiest man to deal with."

"Well, I'll try my best," Nancy said. She and Ann Nordquist chatted with Carson Drew for a few minutes, Ann confirming some of the things the members of Bent Fender had said about Barton—that he tended to be publicity shy, and that he had indeed picked himself up and vanished on two occasions without telling a soul.

"That makes finding him all the more difficult," Nancy told her, "because if he has been kidnapped, there are going to be plenty of people who won't believe it."

"Like the little boy who cried wolf," Carson Drew supplied.

"Exactly." Nancy stood up to go. "Well, I'll leave you two to do your business. Ms. Nordquist, thank you for your time."

"You're welcome. I hope you can track Barton down quickly. We're all awfully worried about him." Ann Nordquist extended her hand to Nancy. "I hope next time we'll meet under more pleasant circumstances."

"I do too. By the way, would any of the people on this list fit these descriptions? A tall, heavyset man with straight dark hair, but balding slightly. Or a shorter man with dark wavy hair, possibly wearing a gold ring in the shape of a dragon or sea monster?" Nancy looked up from her notes on the two men who had been seen backstage.

Ann Nordquist thought for a few seconds. "I don't believe so. No." She shook her head.

"Okay. Well, thanks again." Nancy said goodbye and walked the ten blocks to World Communications' offices. Normally, she would have been thrilled to be on the streets of New York, watching the stream of people and window shopping, but that day she walked quickly, her mind on Barton Novak as she weaved through the crowds. Had he been kidnapped, as Roger Gold suspected, or had he gone on his own, as the rest of the band seemed to think?

Soon, World Communications loomed up in front of her, an imposing steel and glass tower with uniformed guards at the door. *Not again,* Nancy thought, recalling the guards at Radio City Music Hall. She prepared a little speech, but was surprised when the guards let her in with no trouble. In fact, though she found out no new information about Barton, the people at the company were happy to answer her questions. That is, until she got to the last person on the list Ann Nordquist had given her—Harold Marshall.

She opened the door with his name on it and found herself standing before a stylish, sharp-featured young woman of about her own age. The woman's dark hair gleamed with henna-red highlights, and her blue sweater was cut low in the front.

"Yes?" The woman looked up from her desk.

"I'd like to see Mr. Marshall, please." Nancy smiled.

The young woman did not smile back. "Do you have an appointment?"

"No, but I'd like to speak with him about Barton Novak."

"Barton?"

"I'm investigating his disappearance."

"Mr. Marshall is a very busy man, Miss—"

"Drew. Nancy Drew." Nancy extended her hand.

The young woman barely touched it. "I'm afraid he's all booked up today."

"Could it be that he has something to hide?" Nancy suggested, surprised at her own brazenness. When she got no response, she moved toward the inner door and pushed it open.

"Hey, what are you doing? You can't go in there!" the secretary announced, following behind.

"I've already done it," Nancy replied. She found herself facing a small, wiry man with a brown mustache and glasses, who was sitting behind an enormous desk. "Hello, Mr. Marshall."

"Who are you?" He released a cloud of noxious cigar smoke as he spoke. "Vivian, what's she doing here? I gave specific instructions that—"

"I'm sorry, Mr. Marshall," Vivian said, her voice taking on a honey-sweet tone, "but she barged right in here. I couldn't stop her. Please don't be angry."

Harold Marshall's expression softened for a split second. "Oh, Vivian, of course it's not your fault. I didn't mean to snap at you." Nancy watched him. "But as for you—Miss Drew, did you say?" His expression changed to a sneer as he turned back to Nancy. "What is so important that you felt you could waltz right in here? First, my office is invaded by an idiot who thinks that just because he banged out a couple of Barton Novak's riffs last night we must be dying to cut a record—"

"Alan?" Nancy groaned out loud. So poor Alan, filled with dreams of glory, had come face to face with Harold Marshall. Nancy's heart went out to him and to Bess.

"You're a friend of his? Look, I told him no dice, and I mean it. Now, if you'll excuse me . . ." Marshall swiveled around in his chair.

"I am a friend of Alan's, but that's not why I'm here. I'm a detective, and I must ask you a few questions about Barton Novak. Ann Nordquist said you handle his band."

Marshall spun back around, puffing on his cigar. "Ann Nordquist is a pushy dame."

"You mean you don't handle Bent Fender?" Nancy asked.

"I didn't say that. Oh, all right. Go ahead and ask your questions. But be quick about it. I have more important things to do than chat away the morning with someone who calls herself a detective."

Nancy felt her face flush with anger, but she tried to stay calm. "Mr. Marshall, suppose you tell me everything you can about Barton's disappearance."

"Disappearance! Hah!" he snorted. "I hate to

disappoint you, Miss Drew. I know how excited you must be about solving this mystery." His voice oozed sarcasm. "But Barton Novak is safe and sound."

"He is?" Nancy's emotions were a confused jumble of astonishment, relief, and disbelief. "What do you mean?"

"Publicity." George Marshall pronounced the word as if it were an explanation in itself.

"I don't understand."

"It's a publicity gimmick. News like this is certain to boost sales on Fender's most recent album. It's been done plenty of times before. Remember the rumor after the Beatles released *Abbey Road?* That Paul McCartney had died? No, you were probably in diapers back then."

"I *do* know what you're talking about," Nancy countered. She couldn't imagine a rock-and-roll fan who hadn't just about memorized the history of the Beatles. "The record buyers kept thinking they saw clues about it on the album cover and in the lyrics to the songs, isn't that right?"

"The girl detective gets an A plus," Marshall said snidely.

"So you mean Barton's disappearance was engineered?" Nancy shook the newspaper in anger, the realization of what Marshall had done washing over her like a tidal wave. "Why didn't you tell anyone? The rest of the band members are either furious or scared stiff about him."

"Hey," Harold Marshall drawled. "That anger

and fear bought us four-inch headlines. If we'd told them, their reactions wouldn't have been so . . . real." He allowed himself a satisfied smile.

"That's a rotten, inhuman trick," Nancy exclaimed.

"Kid, this is business. What counts is what sells records." Marshall shrugged. "Those fans are going to go wild when they think Barton's gone. They'll start looking for clues in the records, the rock videos. . . . All teens think they're detectives, as you well understand," he added condescendingly.

Nancy bristled. "What I understand is that you think it's good business to lie to Bent Fender's fans. Either that, or to lie to me."

"Look, Miss Drew, if you don't believe what I've told you about Barton, that's your problem. Anybody find a ransom note?"

"No," admitted Nancy, fighting back the urge to grab the mug of coffee on his desk and fling it in his face. "But couldn't you tell the rest of Bent Fender where Barton is, just for their own peace of mind?"

"Let's get something straight." Harold Marshall's lips thinned. "We're sitting on a publicity gold mine here. I only told you what's really happening so you'd stop wasting my time. If you go to the press with anything I said, I'll deny it. Who do you think they'll believe—me, or some kid playing detective?"

He stared at Nancy, challenging her. "As for

Barton, he's a big boy. He could call the band members to tell them he's okay—if he wanted. Maybe he wants some privacy. Think of this as kind of a vacation for him. And do us both a favor. Keep your mouth shut about this whole business."

Nancy didn't like Harold Marshall's tone, but she had to admit to herself that what he was saying jived with everything she'd heard about Barton's thirst for privacy. "Maybe," she said. "But wasn't it strange to pull off this stunt right before the biggest of the 'Rock for Relief' concerts?"

"More publicity that way. Now, if we're all finished here, you can show yourself out."

Nancy took a few steps toward the door, where Vivian, who had stood there all the time, put an insistent hand on Nancy's arm. The interview was clearly over.

"Oh, just one more thing, Mr. Marshall." Nancy turned in the doorway. She asked if he'd ever seen the two men described to her by the Radio City guard.

Marshall shrugged. "How am I supposed to keep track of everyone who goes in and out of this place?"

Did I expect any other answer? Nancy asked herself, leaving Harold Marshall's office without further conversation. She found her way back to the elevator banks, rode down to the main floor, and walked past the indoor fountain and the greenery that adorned the lobby, into the crisp midday sunshine.

Her head swam with conflicting thoughts as she made her way back to the hotel to meet George for lunch. Harold Marshall was one of the rudest, most self-important people she had ever met. But he was just the kind of person to cook up a sneaky publicity trick like the one he'd described. And the fact that no ransom note had been received would suggest that Barton hadn't been kidnapped.

But what about the two mysterious men at the Music Hall and all the clues Nancy had discovered outside Barton's dressing room? Marshall's publicity scheme didn't explain them.

And it didn't explain something else, Nancy thought. *That attack on me last night was no stunt. It was serious—deadly serious.*

Chapter Five

"GEORGE, CAN YOU think of any reason why Harold Marshall would want his biggest star out of the way?" Nancy asked, helping herself to a breadstick.

"How do you know he's not telling the truth?" George held down her napkin as a breeze drifted across the outdoor table at the café where the two girls were having lunch.

"I *don't* know. That's the trouble. It's so confusing. But George, even if Barton isn't in trouble, I'm absolutely convinced that something fishy is going on." Nancy rubbed the back of her head as proof. "But how am I supposed to know where to look when I don't even know what I'm looking for?"

"You tell me, Nan. You're the detective."

"All I do know is that Harold Marshall is creepy. Poor Alan, getting his dream shattered by that goon."

"Well, someone was going to do it sooner or later. That concert last night really put stars in his eyes. I mean, he's acting totally blind as far as realistic expectations go." George leaned over sideways to allow the waiter to put down a bacon cheeseburger in front of each girl and a basket of french fries between them. "Thank you," George said, reaching for a fry. "Anyway," she continued, "Bess isn't helping matters. The way she's been talking, you'd think Alan was going to be the next Bruce Springsteen."

"Well, it's pretty obvious that Harold Marshall cleared up that misconception quickly."

"Mind if we join you?" Nancy heard a familiar voice behind her. She turned around to find Bess and Alan, both smiling broadly.

"Hi! What are you guys doing here? Bess, you said you and Alan were going to have lunch together somewhere."

"We were, but we stopped off at the hotel first and got the most incredible news. We just had to tell you. The hotel manager said he'd recommended this place." Bess plopped down in an empty seat beside Nancy. Alan sat next to George.

"So what's happening?" Nancy asked, noting the looks of pure happiness on their faces. She was more than ready to hear some good news.

"They've decided that—" Bess and Alan both began speaking at once.

Bess laughed. "You go ahead and tell them, Alan. It's your news."

"Well, Vivian from the record company called," Alan said breathlessly, "and they've decided they want me to cut an album for them!"

"What?" Nancy couldn't believe what she was hearing. "But I saw Harold Marshall after you did and he said . . ." Her voice trailed off. There was no point in repeating what would only hurt Alan.

"I know what he said." Alan nodded. "But he must have changed his mind. There was a message from Vivian waiting for us when we got back to the hotel. I returned her call, and she told me to come right over to World Communications. Mr. Marshall wanted to congratulate me in person!"

"What made him change his mind?" Nancy could picture the sneer on George Marshall's lips as he mentioned Alan. She wouldn't have expected him to change his mind for all the gold in Fort Knox.

"I think it had something to do with Barton," Alan said.

"Barton!" Nancy sat straight up in her chair.

"Yeah, that's the other piece of great news," Bess put in. "Alan saw him!"

"When? Where?" Nancy's head swam.

"Right after I went back to Marshall's office. Barton wanted to thank me for filling in for him, and he asked me to do his next couple of gigs while he stays out of the public eye for a while."

"You're kidding," Nancy said.

"Nope. He was hanging around, waiting for a limo to take him to his beach house, that purple bandanna around his neck, sitting in an armchair drinking a beer and watching some movie on a VCR." Alan leaned back in his chair with a happy sigh. "I guess he sort of coaxed Marshall into signing me on. And to think that until yesterday Barton was just someone I dreamed about meeting!"

"Nan, George, isn't it unbelievable?" Bess leaned over and grabbed Nancy's arm.

"Unbelievable," Nancy echoed, meaning it more literally than Bess had. Was she to believe that Harold Marshall had so completely changed his mind about Alan? Or that the only person Barton Novak had asked to see was not a member of his own band, not a close friend or relative, but a fan he'd spoken with for no more than a few minutes?

"Alan, are you *sure* about this?" she asked.

"Sure I'm sure." Alan grinned, his brown eyes shining. "Bess and I are going over to get a tour of the recording studios later this afternoon, and

Marshall's having Vivian draw the contracts up this week. So let's celebrate! Lunch is on me!"

The food was wonderful, and the weather at the outdoor patio was perfect, but throughout the rest of the meal, Nancy's thoughts spun. If Barton was fine, there was no mystery at all, was there? But what about the wallet and the two mysterious men? And what about Harold Marshall's offer to Alan? Just that morning, Marshall was calling Alan an idiot who "banged out a couple of Barton Novak's riffs." Now he was signing a record contract with him.

Nancy had an uncomfortable feeling in the pit of her stomach. Something was very wrong. But she kept her thoughts to herself until after Bess and Alan had left for World Communications. It wasn't until she and George were on their way back to the hotel that she confided her feelings.

"George, don't you think Alan's announcement was kind of, well, weird?"

"What do you mean, Nancy?"

"I mean, everything's happening so fast. One day Alan's taking guitar lessons in River Heights, and the next day he's signing a solo recording contract with one of the biggest labels in the business. George, we both know Alan's got a lot of talent, but this is just a little too much for me to believe."

"What's not to believe? By the end of the week, Alan's going to have a World Communications recording contract in his hands!" George was matter-of-fact. "I mean, it is pretty wild, but it's true."

"I don't know. What if Harold Marshall is stringing Alan along? I don't like that man."

"You think he might not come through?" George asked. "Then why would he make the offer in the first place?"

"I wish I could tell you." Nancy flung her hands up in despair. "I keep trying to get answers on this case, but all I get are more questions."

"And what about Barton?" George voiced one more of those questions as they rounded a corner and came to their hotel.

"Barton—a guy who agrees to disappear right before a concert he's spent months planning. It doesn't figure." Nancy pressed her lips together.

The doorman opened the hotel door, and Nancy and George crossed the tiled lobby floor to the front desk. "Well, what do you intend to do?" George asked.

The clerk on duty handed Nancy and George their keys and also gave Nancy a slip of paper with a telephone message on it. *Carl Rutland, security guard at Radio City Music Hall,* it said. *Found something you might want to know about.* A telephone number was written at the bottom.

"This might answer your question," Nancy told George. "Come on. Let's go up to my room and find out what Mr. Carl Rutland has to say."

* * *

As Nancy fitted her key in the lock, she heard her telephone ringing. "Maybe that's him calling back," she said to George. She pushed the door open and raced for the phone. "Hello?"

"Hi, beautiful," a male voice said.

"Ned! Hi!" Nancy felt herself smile at the sound of Ned Nickerson's mellow baritone. "How are you?"

"Curious, actually. I read in today's paper that Barton Novak vanished right before his concert, and I was wondering what happened. Weren't you supposed to hear Bent Fender play?"

Nancy eased herself onto the edge of the bed. "It's a pretty strange story. At first I was sure Barton had been kidnapped, but now it turns out that it's really just a publicity gimmick. I think. I mean, I don't know what to think. Ned, I don't know if I've got a mystery to solve or not." Nancy's words came out in a fast, nervous rush.

"Nan," Ned said slowly, "slow down and tell me all about it."

Nancy took a deep breath and recounted everything that had happened since her arrival in New York.

When she was done, Ned let out a long, low whistle. "Sounds like you've run into some people who play awfully rough. That blow on the head is serious. I don't like it at all," he said, worry rising with his voice.

"Ned, I'm fine," Nancy assured him. "The

worst part isn't the bump on my head. It's that I don't know if the wallet has anything to do with Barton or the two men backstage, or anything. I'm so keyed up. I don't know whether to forget this business or what."

"Well, how about a consultation?" Ned suggested. "Say, in about two hours? I can get on the road right away."

"You're coming up from school to spend some time with me in New York? Oh, Ned, that sounds great! I'm sure you can share Alan's room with him."

"Alan? You mean Bess's new superstar? The one who was offered the recording contract?"

Nancy frowned. "Yeah, Bess's superstar. And Ned, maybe you can help me figure out what's going on here."

"I'll do everything I can," Ned promised. "And if anyone tries to knock you over the head again, I'll give them a taste of their own medicine."

"My hero," Nancy giggled. "But don't forget, I'm the one with the brown belt in karate."

"Do you have to remind me?" Ned said, groaning.

"Well, I won't try any of my new moves on you this time," Nancy said solemnly. "Except maybe on the dance floor. Roger Gold is taking us to a wild new club tonight."

"Sounds great."

"Good. It's a date." Before saying goodbye,

Nancy gave Ned the address of the hotel. "There's an indoor parking lot right across the street," she added.

"Well, you look a little happier than you did a few minutes ago," George observed from the couch. "Love, love is the miracle drug," she sang teasingly. It was the refrain of one of Bent Fender's new songs.

"George, do you think Ned's ready to forget about Daryl?" Nancy felt herself blush.

"I don't know, Nan, but a few days together in the most exciting city in the world ought to do *something* for the two of you."

"Hmm. You know, this might turn out to be a good vacation after all. If I could just stop worrying about Barton, and Alan's record contract . . ." Nancy felt herself coming down to earth. "Speaking of which, I better call that security guard back."

She dialed the number on the message sheet. "Hello, is this Carl Rutland?" she asked the man who answered the telephone.

"Speaking."

"Hi, this is Nancy Drew. From the concert last night."

"Oh, Miss Drew. Yes. Hello."

"You said you found something?"

"That's right. Well, first of all, whoever gave you that knock on the head came in and out by the fire escape, off one of the dance studios. When I checked the windows leading out to it, I found that one of the latches had been forced open, and we always keep them locked."

"Mr. Rutland, do you think someone would go through all the trouble of climbing the fire escape and breaking in just to steal a wallet?" Nancy asked.

"Maybe. But it would be very risky. There are too many people around the Music Hall when there's a rock concert. You know, fans come without tickets and try to scalp them or just sneak in, and they wind up hanging around outside. Anyway, there'd be too good a chance of being caught."

"Then," Nancy mused aloud, "there must have been something worth far more than money in that wallet. Well, thank you for the information, Mr. Rutland."

"Wait, that's not the only thing I wanted to tell you," Carl Rutland said. "I found something outside Barton Novak's dressing room, near all those boxes and things."

"You did?" Nancy was alert.

"Yeah. A scarf. A violet-colored scarf with designs on it."

"Mr. Rutland," Nancy said hoarsely, in a flash of understanding, "you mean you found a purple bandanna—a square of heavy cotton, with a sort of leafy pattern stitched on it in green?"

"Yeah, that's it. Is it yours?"

"No. No, it's Barton Novak's, sort of his good luck charm," Nancy said, "and one of a kind.

His sister did the embroidery." Nancy remembered reading that in several articles about Barton. "He never plays a concert without it. Um, Mr. Rutland, when did you say you found the bandanna?"

"Last night, after they took you home. I've got it right here in my pocket."

"Last night?" Nancy's brain was working overtime. "Well, just hold on to it. I'll make arrangements to get it from you." Nancy thanked the man again and got off the phone in a hurry, her hand trembling as she hung up the receiver.

"Nancy, what's the matter? You look like that security guard has been telling you ghost stories or something," George said.

"No, not ghost stories. Something much more real and much more frightening. It's Alan, George. He's been lying to us!"

Chapter Six

GEORGE'S EYES WIDENED. "What do you mean?"

"That guard found Barton's bandanna," Nancy explained.

"So? Maybe he dropped it without realizing."

"But don't you see?" Nancy felt sick at the realization. "Just this morning, Alan told us he saw Barton. And he said that Barton was wearing that bandanna!"

George began to look sick too. "Oh no."

"Even if he was a little flaky, I always thought I could trust Alan," Nancy said. "But now I don't know *what* he's gotten into—except that it's really dangerous." She got up and headed for the door.

"Hey, where are we going?" George grabbed a sweater from the bed.

"To find Alan." Nancy slipped on her jeans jacket and took the room key. "He and Bess must be getting their tour of the World recording studios right now." She put an insistent hand on George's back and moved her toward the door.

"Wouldn't it be easier to call him there?" George suggested.

Nancy shook her head vigorously. "No way. What if they wind up putting us through to Vivian or Mr. Marshall's office? I don't want them to know anything about this. I want to get Alan alone. Besides, I need to see the expression on his face when we confront him with his lie. It would be worth a thousand words, as they say." Nancy stepped out of the room.

George followed, a worried look in her brown eyes. "Nancy, do you think Bess knows Alan's lying? I mean, it seems so impossible—"

"I know. Bess has never been anything less than a hundred percent straight with us. I'm sure she wouldn't hold anything back. One thing really scares me, though. If Alan isn't the kind of guy we think he is, Bess could be in trouble." Nancy locked the room and headed for the elevator, with George a few steps behind her.

"But, Nancy, it's so obvious that the guy is

nuts about Bess. And don't forget, he helped us solve your last mystery."

"I know. I only hope he's got a good explanation for this."

Finding Alan turned out to be easier said than done. When Nancy and George arrived at World Communications, the receptionist told them that the recording facilities were not housed in the same building as the executive offices. "Our recording is done by an independent company. Oraye Sound." She wrote down Oraye's address.

"Is it far from here?" Nancy asked.

"All the way downtown."

Nancy took that to mean yes. "Come on, George. It looks like you and I are going for a little cab ride."

They raced outside and hailed a taxi. "205 East Fourth Street," Nancy told the driver. "And go whatever way's the fastest. It's important."

"Lady, it's always important. Everyone in this town is always in a hurry," the taxi driver responded. "But I'll do my best. Of course, going through midtown this time of day, there's always traffic."

"Isn't there some way to avoid it?" George asked. "This really is an emergency."

"Then you shoulda chartered a helicopter." The driver swung out into the flow of cars, inches in front of a gray hatchback. The driver of the gray car let out an angry blast of his horn.

"Oh brother," grumbled Nancy a few minutes later, looking nervously at her watch. "We could walk faster than this." She pulled several crinkled dollar bills out of her jacket pocket. "We'll get out here," she announced, before they had reached their destination. She pushed the money through the opening in the Plexiglas shield that separated the driver from his passengers. "Keep the change."

The taxi came to a halt, and she jumped out. "Come on, George. Maybe we can still make it down there before Bess and Alan leave."

The girls reached East Fourth Street in record time. "We should have recruited you for girls' track in high school," George panted.

Nancy wiped her forehead. "Let's see," she said, trying to catch her breath, "194, 196 . . . It must be on the other side of the street. 201. Yeah, there it is, 205."

Nancy rang the buzzer for Oraye Sound, Inc., and she and George entered the building and headed for the fifth floor. The elevator opened on a large area divided into a number of work spaces by movable partitions. Several halls branched off in different directions from the central space. People rushed back and forth busily, and the hum of voices filled the room. In one corner was a large desk that was not hidden behind any of the dividers; a young man sat behind it, typing.

Nancy and George approached him, and Nancy cleared her throat. He looked up from his typewriter. "Hi, are you with the NYU group?" he asked. "You're late," he continued, without waiting for an answer. "The tour's started already. They're down that way, in one of the editing rooms."

"NYU?" Nancy asked.

"Yes. New York University. Aren't you film students?"

Nancy shook her head. "Actually, we're here looking for our friends, Alan Wales and Bess Marvin."

"Who?"

"They should have come in early this afternoon. He's medium height with frizzy brown hair. She has blond hair a little past her shoulders, and she's on the short side," George supplied.

The man thought for a moment. "Oh, you mean the two Harold Marshall sent over."

Nancy's brow furrowed at Mr. Marshall's name. "Yes. That's right."

"Oh, you just missed them. They were talking about going out to celebrate something."

Nancy felt thoroughly frustrated as she and George started back across the large room. "George," she said, in what was for her a down voice. "What's going on with this case? I feel as if I'm following shadows, not leads." Now she wouldn't be able to get hold of Alan until their rendezvous at the club that evening. She'd lose several hours of sleuthing time—hours that could be critical to Barton Novak.

Before George could reply, Nancy saw something that made her pulse speed up. Moving as quickly as she could, she pulled George into an unoccupied work space. "It's Vivian!" she whispered, peeking out from around the partition.

"Who?"

"Harold Marshall's secretary." Nancy watched as Vivian emerged from the stairwell carrying a bulky package under her arm. The woman glanced around furtively and slipped down one of the hallways. The young man at the corner desk, his back to the work spaces and network of halls, continued to type, and Vivian passed by unnoticed.

"Looks to me like she's sneaking around," George said.

"Come on," Nancy urged. "Maybe the trip down here won't be a waste after all." She grabbed George's elbow, and silently, keeping a safe distance behind her, the girls followed Vivian down the hall.

Vivian seemed to know exactly where she was going. After proceeding along a maze of corridors past numerous doors, she stopped abruptly in front of one of them. Second-guessing the next move, Nancy pulled George back around the last corner in the corridor—and not a second too soon. Nancy edged around the corner just in time to see Vivian whipping her head around, clearly checking to make sure she was alone. Then she entered the room she had stopped in front of.

"Now what?" George hissed as they both breathed a sigh of relief.

"Well, we can't follow her in there," Nancy thought out loud, "so we'll have to wait until she leaves. Then we can see what's in that room. But let's get out of here. She's going to come back this way, and besides, someone might see us."

"Maybe there's a ladies' room around here," George suggested. "We could hide in there until she leaves."

The girls found one a few doors down and entered cautiously, making sure it was unoccupied. Then Nancy posted herself by the door, leaving it open a finger's width so she could peer out.

Vivian didn't take long. Only a few minutes later, Nancy heard the clicking of her high-heeled black pumps on the tiled hallway floor and noticed that Vivian no longer carried the package that had been under her arm. "She must have dropped something off," Nancy said, pulling the restroom door shut as Vivian walked by.

Nancy waited until the footsteps faded. Then she peeked out again. The corridor was empty.

"Okay, *now!*" she instructed George. The two friends made a dash for the room Vivian had entered and let themselves inside, the door opening and closing with a faint squeak.

The walls of the small room were lined, floor to ceiling, with cabinets, and in the middle of the room were low, free-standing, enclosed bins.

"It's some kind of storeroom," Nancy observed.

She pulled at the handle of one of the cabinets —labeled 1981, A through C—and found it locked. She tried one on the adjacent wall. The typed sticker on the door read 1982, G through K. It didn't open either.

George was walking around, fiddling with the cabinet doors. "These are locked too," she said, her words colored with annoyance. Then she called out softly, "Nancy, come look at this."

When Nancy joined her, the young detective took a look at a list George had been studying. It was taped to the wall. The page was divided into columns headed *name, title of master, date borrowed, date returned.*

"Masters. So that's why all these drawers are locked so securely. George, this is where they keep all the original recordings, the ones they copy when they press the albums they sell."

"Right," George said, "I remember back when we were sophomores, this record store in Mount Harmon was closed down because the owner was selling albums that had been made illegally. I'm not sure of the details, but he was buying the albums for way under the normal costs, selling them for the retail prices, and raking in a fortune."

Nancy nodded. "Right. If these masters get into the wrong hands, they can be used to make a lot of illegal money. Record piracy, I think they call it."

As Nancy talked, she skimmed the list in front of her for Vivian's name. It wasn't there. *What was Vivian up to?* she wondered. She guessed that the parcel contained masters Vivian had sneaked out and then sneaked back in. Was Vivian getting them for Harold Marshall so he could mint illegal albums and sell them as the real thing? If so, then Barton was right to wonder about Bent Fender's royalties. They wouldn't earn money on copies sold illegally.

Nancy pondered that, continuing to study the list. Suddenly a familiar name near the bottom of the page caught her eye. "George!" she gasped, pointing to the bold script.

George's gaze followed Nancy's finger. "Oh wow! Barton Novak!"

"And he was here just a few days ago!" Nancy added. "George, I bet Barton came here and discovered something. Maybe he found out that some of the masters were missing!"

"And then someone found out that Barton

knew, and had to make sure he didn't tell anyone."

Nancy nodded, her face taut. "That's a really strong motive. Now I'm sure Barton didn't disappear on his own. He must have been kidnapped!"

Chapter Seven

THE PIECES OF the puzzle were finally beginning to fall into place. "This explains why there was no ransom note," Nancy continued. "Barton's kidnappers weren't interested in getting money, just in keeping him from spilling the beans. I bet all this has something to do with his wanting to talk to me after the concert." Nancy leaned back against one of the cabinets, digesting the implications of the new discovery.

Suddenly, a thought occurred to her that made her blood go colder than an arctic ice floe. "George," she said, "if Barton's kidnappers don't want a ransom for him, maybe they don't intend to free him at all."

George's ruddy complexion drained to pale.

The two girls stood in silence, the horrible realization sinking in until the stillness in the room was shattered by the soft but unmistakable squeal of the door opening. Nancy gasped.

A sandy-haired man with a mustache stepped inside. There was no place to escape his gaze in the small room. "Who are you?" he asked gruffly. "No unauthorized personnel allowed in here."

Nancy thought quickly. "We, um . . . we're with the NYU group."

"Film students," George added, backing up Nancy's story.

"Oh. Well, what are you kids doing in here? Your group is over in one of the editing rooms." He motioned for them to leave. "Down this hall and to the left."

For a moment, Nancy was flooded with a sense of relief. "Oh. Thank you, sir." She and George moved toward the door.

But as soon as they were safely out of Oraye Sound and outside again, Nancy's relief dissolved in a flood of nerves. What if she couldn't locate Barton before it was too late? Or was it already too late? Who was at the bottom of the sordid mess, and how much did Alan know about it? How safe was Bess if she inadvertently had been caught smack in the middle of a record pirating conspiracy?

Stop! Nancy admonished herself. Standing in the middle of a busy New York street thinking about all this wasn't going to get her any closer to answering the questions that were gnawing at her. She took several breaths, taking the air deep into her body and breathing from her stomach, the way she'd been taught in karate class.

"Okay," she told George, "the first thing to do is to find out which people have access to the room with the masters in it, and then find out what they know." Nancy made a beeline for the nearest pay phone, fishing around in her jeans pocket as she ran.

A loud, jarring crackle came out of the earpiece as she picked up the receiver. "Broken." She slammed down the phone and moved over to the next one. "Good," she told George. "This one's got a dial tone." She pulled her little notebook out of her shoulder bag and quickly turned the pages until she found Roger Gold's number.

Be home. Please be home. She punched out his number on the pushbutton telephone.

"Hello?" Roger's voice came over the wire.

"Roger. It's Nancy Drew. Thank goodness you're there."

"Nancy, what's wrong? Is it about Barton? Do you know where he is?"

"Not yet," Nancy replied, trying to keep from sounding frightened, "but I think I've got my first solid lead."

"Was he kidnapped?" Roger sounded nervous.

"Yes, I think so."

"I knew it! No way did Barton go off on his own. He was too involved in those concerts." Roger paused. "So what do you think's going on?"

"I think someone's pirating Bent Fender's records. And probably other groups' records, too."

"Pirating our records?" A string of angry words streamed out of Roger Gold's normally soft-speaking mouth. Nancy waited for him to calm down. "I'm sorry," he said finally. "Listening to me get mad isn't going to help Barton, is it?"

"That's okay, Roger. I'm not exactly a bearer of good tidings. But there is something you can tell me that will help get to the bottom of this."

"Anything."

"Who has access to the cabinets in the masters room at Oraye Sound?"

"Well, all the techies—the recording technicians—at Oraye, for starters. And they usually give a key to the musicians who record there."

"Like you and Barton and the rest of the band?"

"Right. I mean, we do most of our work at our own private studios, but we do some mixing and stuff there sometimes. Yeah."

"Anyone else?" Nancy asked.

"The top executives at World," Roger said.

"Harold Marshall?"

A moment of silence, then Roger exploded. "Is that creep in on Barton's disappearance?"

"Well, he has an interesting reason for why Barton didn't make the concert."

"I don't buy it," Roger said firmly, after hearing Harold Marshall's story. "Barton would want the sales of our records to center around our music, not around gossip about where he is. Besides, he doesn't like the idea of people poking around in his private life. Nope. Marshall's story just doesn't make sense."

Nancy wasn't surprised by Roger's opinion. Marshall's story had too many holes in it for her to swallow it completely. "Roger, thank you. You've been a big help. Oh, and one more thing. How does Harold Marshall get along with his secretary?"

"Vivian? They're a perfect team. The witch and the warlock. Marshall thinks she's the greatest thing since stereophonic sound. The rat has had his eye on her since the day she came to work for him. And she'll do anything he asks. And I mean anything."

"Roger, would Vivian do Marshall's dirty work?" Nancy pictured Vivian sneaking into the masters room.

"Sure."

"And would Marshall be low enough to pirate his own company's records and pocket the profit?"

"That toad is low enough to do anything," Roger answered.

"You know, it's possible that we might have our man," Nancy said. "But we have to catch him in the act to make sure."

"You just tell me what I have to do to help," Roger offered. "I'd be only too happy to nail that bum."

"The best thing you can do is act as if nothing's happened. Meet us at the club tonight, work on your new songs, do whatever you would normally do. We don't want Marshall to think we're on to him." Nancy inhaled sharply. "Because if Barton's disappearance is any indication, what we know could be hazardous to our health!"

She hung up the phone and looked at George. "Come on. We've got to find out a lot more before we crack this case."

"Action!" George rubbed her hands together. "This is the part I like the best."

Nancy shook her head. "I'm not so sure this is action you'll enjoy . . ."

"Ugh. I feel like I'm back in school again," George moaned.

"School was never a life-or-death situation," Nancy responded gravely. "Now read."

The girls were seated in the research room of the Jefferson Market Library, a brisk walk from the studios of Oraye Sound. Books and back copies of magazines were piled next to them on the old wooden tables.

Nancy skimmed through an article in *Allegro,* the monthly newspaper of the musicians' union. "George, listen to this." She read out loud, keeping her voice low, so as not to disturb the people around her. " 'One billion dollars per year are lost in residuals, due to pirated sound and video recordings in the United States and abroad.' One billion dollars worth of royalty money! Can you believe that?" she exclaimed. "Wow, I had no idea what a huge black market there is for pirated recordings. There's certainly enough money at stake to make some crook want to get rid of anyone in the way."

Nancy's stomach did a slow somersault as she thought about Barton's safety.

"Nancy, here's something," George whispered a moment later. "Certain countries have no copyright laws at all. They simply obtain existing printed or recorded materials from other countries and publish or manufacture copies of their own, or they purchase pirated copies at a cost far below the market value. No revenue from these sales goes to the artist or company that holds the copyright."

Nancy listened intently. "Wow! You mean somebody could take records that were made illegally here and sell them in certain other places where there are no copyright laws?"

"Right."

"And these foreign governments wouldn't consider it a crime?"

George nodded and continued, her brown-eyed gaze gliding across the page as she read. "The one major country to operate without copyright laws is the People's Republic of China."

"China!" A bell went off in Nancy's head. "George, that wallet I found backstage during the concert—it had a dragon on it—a Chinese dragon! I wonder if that's more than just a coincidence." Nancy rested her elbow on the table and propped her chin on the palm of her hand.

"Do you think Harold Marshall might have some connection to the Chinese?" George asked. "Or Vivian? Somehow, I can't imagine her trudging through rice paddies in those high-heeled shoes." George let out a giggle, despite the severity of the situation. Then she clapped a hand over her mouth. "Sorry, Nan."

But Nancy wasn't at all annoyed with George. "You're a genius!" she said excitedly, trying at the same time to keep her voice down. "Maybe Vivian wouldn't be able to wing it on a tour of the rice fields, but I know someone who would."

"Nancy, what are you talking about?"

"That picture you had of Vivian reminded me of a poster I saw of Chinese workers harvesting rice. I saw it just this morning . . . hanging on the wall in Ann Nordquist's office!" Nancy grabbed George's arm. "Ann is Bent Fender's agent. And she just came back from China. She was telling my dad and me about her trip." Nancy's pulse was racing. "What if that wallet belongs to her? And what if she wasn't just sight-seeing?"

"But what about Mr. Marshall?" George reminded her.

"Yes, then there's Harold Marshall." Nancy pondered that for a few moments. "You know, he and Ann Nordquist both made a point of telling me how much they disliked each other. But what if they did that just to throw me off the track? It's possible they're working together."

"But Nancy, you told me that Ann Nordquist seemed like a nice woman."

"She did. I mean, she does. I liked her. And I don't see why she would own a wallet with the initial L. Still, I don't think we can rule her out entirely. You can never be too sure."

"I guess not. We thought Alan was playing straight with us, and look what happened. If he drags Bess into this, he's going to be really sorry."

Nancy nodded. "Speaking of which, let's get back to the hotel. I want to pick up Ned and get to the club. Bess's wonder boy and I are in for a little heart-to-heart." She gathered up the books and bound volumes of magazines and began replacing them on the shelves. "And," she added, "I think I ought to do a little checking up on Ms. Ann Nordquist."

"Yeah," George said. "Maybe she got tired of earning her ten percent and decided to make a real killing."

"I hope it hasn't gone that far." Nancy hesitated before going on. ". . . As far as murder."

Chapter Eight

NED!" NANCY THREW her arms around the tall, broad-shouldered young man. "Sorry to keep you waiting. Have you been here long?" Nancy had found Ned sitting on the plush velvet sofa in the hotel lobby.

"Got here just about five minutes ago," Ned said, bending down to give her a powerful hug. A lock of thick dark hair fell forward over his eye, and Nancy brushed it away.

"I want you to know," she said, her mind still reeling from her frenzied afternoon, "your visit is the one bright spot in this entire trip."

"Uh-oh. Sounds like my favorite detective is

wrapped up in a tough case. What's happened since we talked on the phone?"

Nancy let out a sigh. "First I had so few real clues that I didn't even know if I had a mystery or not. Now, all of a sudden, there are all sorts of leads . . . and I don't know which ones to follow first." Nancy could see George coming across the lobby with the room keys she had picked up from the front desk. "Listen, why don't you come upstairs, and I'll tell you everything?"

A few minutes later, the three friends were seated around the table in the main room of the suite, drinking the Cokes they had ordered from room service. Nancy and George recounted the day's events, from the newspaper headlines about Barton to their library research.

Ned looked thoughtful. "So you think the trail of evidence could lead to that record producer—"

"Harold Marshall," George supplied.

"Right, or the Nordquist woman, or even Alan?" Ned's voice dropped as he uttered Bess's boyfriend's name. "So, I'm sharing a room with one of your suspects, Nancy?"

Nancy shrugged. "I haven't even seen Alan since you called, so I haven't had a chance to ask him about sharing his room. And once I confront him about his lie, I'm not sure how generous he's going to feel about doing any favors for my friends." Nancy twisted a strand of hair around her index finger. "But don't worry. There's a couch in Dad's room. I'm sure he wouldn't mind having you stay with us."

As if on cue, the door to the suite opened, and Carson Drew stepped inside. "Ned! Well, hello. I thought I heard your voice. It's good to see you again."

Ned stood up, and they shook hands. "Good to be here, Mr. Drew."

"So." Carson Drew turned toward his daughter and George. "Anything new on the case?"

"As a matter of fact, Dad, yes. I was wondering if you could arrange another meeting between me and Ann Nordquist. I need to talk to her."

"I'm sure she'd be happy to. In fact, I'll ask her tonight at dinner."

"You mean you're having another business meeting?" Nancy wondered if she should tell her father that Ann Nordquist was on her list of suspects. No, she decided. She'd keep it to herself until she had more information.

Carson Drew liked to tease his daughter, to remind her that her detective's methods were a direct contrast to his own lawyer's procedure.

"Not exactly," he replied. "Actually, I asked her to dine with me more for pleasure."

Nancy felt a chill race through her. "For pleasure?" she echoed dully. Normally she would have been happy that her father had a dinner date. Her mother had died when she was a very little girl, and she felt it had been too long that her father had done without female companionship. He dated occasionally, but for the most part, when he had free time, he threw himself into extra work projects. But Ann Nordquist? The woman had seemed nice, but Nancy couldn't get the China connection out of her mind.

"Yes, for pleasure." Carson Drew chuckled. "Your old father deserves to enjoy himself occasionally. And I find Ann Nordquist a very attractive, highly intelligent woman."

Nancy swallowed hard. "Oh," she said, exchanging looks with George and Ned. "Well, I—I hope you have fun." Her voice came out in a high, tight squeak. What if her father were going out with one of Barton Novak's kidnappers?

"Psycho killer . . ." Vintage rock blared from the speakers, and dancers spun beneath the ultraviolet lights. The club was a study in downtown funk. A stage had been set up at the front, and the people milling around in the crowded room ranged from the utmost in fashionable to the totally outrageous.

"Wow! Check *that* get-up," Ned said, tapping Nancy on the arm.

A girl with a rainbow-colored bristle of hair walked by the table where they sat, her slender body draped in black satin and lace.

"What? Oh, yeah, I see her," Nancy replied distractedly, glancing at the girl for only a brief second. Quickly, she turned her attention back to the entrance of the club, which was visible from her balcony perch. The second Alan and Bess walked through that doorway, she wanted to know about it.

"Nan, they'll be here soon," Ned assured her gently. "Meanwhile, you might as well enjoy yourself. How often do you get to come to a place like this?" He reached out and trailed his fingers up her back.

Nancy could feel the electric tingle of his touch. She inched her chair closer to his and rested her head on his shoulder, the softness of his sweater caressing her cheek. "Oh, Ned, I'm sorry. I guess I'm not a very good date."

"You're the best. I just wish I could do something to cheer you up."

"Ned, sometimes I don't think I deserve you. You come all the way from school to be with me, and I'm so wrapped up in this case I'm no fun at all."

"Hey, it's okay. This is me, remember? I've stuck by you during lots of tough cases. I know what you're going through."

Nancy lifted her head and looked into Ned's brown eyes, her gaze holding his. "You're not mad at me, are you, about what happened on the last case?"

She couldn't quite bring herself to pronounce Daryl's name. Sure, she'd been a willing victim of Daryl's sexy eyes and smooth personality, but it had been Ned who'd bailed her out of a dangerous situation during that case, and Ned who had been there for her once the criminals were safely behind bars.

Ned cupped her face in his large hands. "It hurt, sure. I mean, if it hadn't, I'd have to start wondering how much I really love you. And Nancy, I do love you."

Nancy held her breath, afraid to break the spell of the moment. But when Ned's tender gaze left her face, she followed his glance.

"Alan!" She was on her feet, the tough detective back in top form. "Let's go!"

Nancy and Ned flew down the back staircase and caught up with Alan and Bess at the coat checkroom. The attendant was already hanging up George's coat. She must have gone ahead to check out the dance floor.

"Nan! Hi. And Ned!" Bess gave him an exuberant hug while Alan greeted Nancy easily. "Hi. How're you doing?"

Nancy steeled herself. "I'd be a lot better if I could figure out why you lied to me about seeing Barton Novak."

Bess spun around, looking like she'd just been slapped. "What do you mean?" Her voice rose. "Alan wouldn't lie, would you?" she asked, moving quickly to his side.

Alan looked from Nancy to Bess, and then back to Nancy. "I, ah—"

Bess was gazing up at Alan, who met her eyes

and held her glance for a moment that seemed to go on forever. Nancy watched nervously. She couldn't imagine anything worse than getting caught between them.

"No," Alan said finally, his voice stronger, "of course I wouldn't lie."

"You told me you saw Barton wearing his purple bandanna," Nancy said accusingly.

"That's right."

"Alan, the security guard at Radio City Music Hall found Barton's bandanna last night after we left. He's had it ever since."

Alan's cheeks blazed under the colored lights. "Well, maybe . . . maybe there are two bandannas."

Nancy felt a rush of annoyance. Why was Alan playing games with her? "You know as well as I do that it's a one-of-a-kind good luck charm. Every article written about Barton mentions that."

Alan shifted from one foot to the other. Bess's gaze was still frozen on him. "So, um, suppose I remembered wrong. Suppose he wasn't wearing the bandanna. What's the big deal?" He raised his eyes and looked at Bess, a note of pleading in his voice. "You believe I saw him, don't you?"

"Of course I do," Bess responded. She whirled to face Nancy. "What's gotten into you?" she snapped.

Bess's angry tone stung Nancy like a bitter

wind. "Bess, I don't mean to hurt you, but I don't think Alan is telling the truth. Doesn't it strike you as a little weird that in the last two days, one of the few people to have any contact with Barton Novak is someone who barely knows him? Not even Barton's sister or his best friends have heard from him."

"Why would I lie?" Alan said after what felt like an interminable pause. "I feel kind of like Barton's my brother. I mean, I learned all about rock and roll from listening to him. Now we're even recording on the same label."

"That's just it! Frankly, Alan, your instant success hasn't felt right to me since the second you told me. We all know how good you are, but you're not a professional. Not yet. And World is a label for professionals. You know what I think? I think Harold Marshall offered you that contract in return for throwing me off the scent."

Nancy waited for Alan's response, but it was Bess who jumped forward, her face inches from Nancy's, her hands clenched. *"Nancy Drew!* I thought you were one of my very best friends. What a jerk I was. Alan got that contract on talent. Pure talent. And if you're too dense to realize that, at least you ought to keep your opinions to yourself!" She spun on her heels, grabbing Alan's arm and maneuvering him away. "We don't need to waste our time with people like that," Nancy heard her say.

"Wait, Bess!" Nancy called out frantically. She started after her friend, but Ned put out a restraining hand.

"Nancy, why don't you wait until she's cooled off."

"She's never going to cool off, Ned. Bess is going to hate me forever." Nancy watched her friend storm off, rigid with fury, never once looking back.

Chapter Nine

GEORGE WHIRLED AROUND the dance floor with one partner after another—first Linda Ferrare's cousin, then Jim Parker, and finally a friend Jim had brought with him. Across the room, Bess was also dancing, laughing and clearly making a show of having a wonderful time.

But Nancy's feet seemed to stick to the floor. Her body barely swayed to the song pulsing in the smoky air.

"Nancy, maybe we ought to call it a night," Ned shouted over the loud music.

Nodding her head wearily, Nancy stopped dancing. Ned put his arm around her shoulders and guided her off the floor. "I'll bet Bess doesn't stay mad at you for more than a few hours," he consoled her.

Nancy's glance strayed to Bess and Alan, who were rocking to an old Rolling Stones tune. As if sensing that she was being watched, Bess turned and shot icy daggers with her glance across the crowded room. Then she guided Alan around, leaving Nancy to stare at her back. "I don't know," Nancy said glumly. "Besides, it's not just Bess. It's Barton and the record pirating and my father going out with Ann Nordquist . . ."

"Look, at this point, you don't know if Ann Nordquist is anything more than an enthusiastic tourist, right?" Ned asked. "She might not have anything to do with the pirating at all."

"Maybe not. I mean, she did seem really sweet when I met her, but the Chinese connection is the only plausible link I've been able to turn up so far between that wallet I found and the record scam."

"The key words are 'so far,' Nan. You don't know anything for certain yet. So how about if we head back to the hotel and you try to relax and get a good night's rest. Tomorrow you'll have lots of energy. Maybe you'll be able to crack this case once and for all."

The corners of Nancy's mouth turned up for the first time all evening. "Okay, Mom."

"Just giving you good, sensible advice, my dear," teased Ned in a high voice.

They got their coats and said their goodbyes,

making plans to have breakfast with George the next morning.

"See you in the hotel dining room," George said as Nancy and Ned were leaving. "And Nancy, don't get freaked out about Bess. She'll come around. She loves you to pieces, just like I do."

Nancy gave George a big hug. "Thanks. You're the best."

"Yeah, you're a good friend," Ned agreed, giving George an affectionate pat on the back.

"Hey, hey, please. You don't want me to get a swollen ego, do you?" George winked.

Nancy and Ned headed for the exit. Cool, crisp air greeted Nancy as she stepped outside. She inhaled the night, savoring the relative quiet after the pulsing music and din of voices in the club. The street was dark. Except for a streetlamp down the block, the only source of light was the club's marquee.

"Something catch your eye?" Ned asked.

"No. Just thinking what this street must look like in the daytime. Pretty dingy, I guess." Nancy's eyes slowly gazed up and down the street.

"Yeah, there's some difference between the junk piled out here and the way the club's fixed up." Ned's hand gently took hold of Nancy's. "Do you want to walk for a while? It may be seedy down here, but I don't think it's dangerous."

Nancy smiled. Maybe now was a good time for

them to work on their relationship. "I'd love a walk with you, Ned. Dangerous or not."

Ned could feel the sincerity in her words. Slowly he leaned forward to kiss her.

"Ned? Ned Nickerson?" The mood was broken by a short young man who was leaving the club behind them. He rushed up to them, brushing his wavy brown hair out of one eye.

Ned took a hard look at him. "Dave, isn't it?"

"Yeah. Dave Peck. Long time no see, buddy." Dave stuck out a leather-gloved hand, and Nancy could see a thick gold chain bracelet studded with gems that sparkled under the streetlights.

Ned grasped Dave's hand in his. "Yes . . . a long time. I guess I didn't recognize you all . . . all dressed up."

"Yup. Great new threads, don't you think?" Dave patted his leather jacket, which was decorated with tucks and folds and numerous zippers. He wore it open, revealing a short, muscular body in a pair of beige slacks and a silk shirt, several of the top buttons open to show off more gold jewelry. On his feet were a pair of green snakeskin cowboy boots.

"Oh, Nancy, this is Dave Peck. We know each other from school. Dave, my girlfriend, Nancy."

"Hello," Nancy said, trying to imagine Dave at Emerson College. Somehow she couldn't quite picture him burning the midnight oil. At least not over books.

As Dave turned toward her, the smile on his

face slipped away. He stared at her with his mouth open, his eyes wide, as if she were a frightening vision from the past.

"Is something wrong?" Nancy asked.

Dave gave his head a hard shake. "Oh . . . no. No, I'm happy to meet you." He grasped her hand, and through his tight gloves Nancy could feel a large ring on one finger. "Any pal of Nickerson's is a pal of mine." He turned his attention back to Ned. "So, what's happening?"

"The usual," Ned responded politely. "Studying, going to classes. Midterms are coming up in a few weeks."

"So, you're just in town for a vacation?"

Ned nodded. "We had Friday off because Emerson is hosting an education conference. I decided to spend the three-day weekend here with Nancy. How about you? What are you doing these days?"

Clearly that was the question Dave had been waiting for. "Man, I've got to tell you, dropping out of school was the best thing I ever did."

So that's his story, Nancy thought.

"Life is great," Dave went on. "Couldn't be better. No more forcing myself to get up in the morning and go to classes. No more tests or papers. I do what I want. Lots of money, lots of chicks." He gave a lewd laugh and flashed Ned a thumbs-up sign. "No offense to the little lady," he added to Nancy.

Nancy gritted her teeth.

"Yup. This is a great town if you're into success. Got myself a great little business."

"You've got your own business?" Ned blurted out.

"Well, actually I've got a—sort of a partner," Dave hedged.

Nancy found herself betting anything that Dave's so-called partner was, in truth, his boss. She could tell that Ned didn't quite buy his story either. Though whatever Dave was doing, it was plain that he did have money to throw around.

"So, what is it you do?" Ned asked, as if reading Nancy's mind. "I wouldn't mind a little extra pocket money," he kidded.

"A little of this, a little of that," Dave replied vaguely. "But I still like to keep up with the rock scene. No better place for it in the world than right here in this city."

"I guess not," Ned said. "Well, it was nice talking to you, Dave. We'd better get going."

"Sure. There's my limo anyhow." Dave pointed to a black stretch limo pulling around the corner and stopping across the street from the club.

"Wow, that's some car." Ned couldn't hide his astonishment.

"She's a beaut, huh?" Dave said smugly. "Well, good bumping into you, pal. Nice to meet you, Nancy." His words were cordial, but Nancy caught the peculiar look in his eye again as he addressed her.

"'Bye, Dave." Nancy watched him go, stepping into the street. She gave a little shudder. Dave was definitely not her idea of a nice guy. And she seemed to make him uncomfortable, too.

"What is it about him?" she said to Ned. "He gives me the creeps."

"Yeah, he's pretty weird. Truth is, he didn't drop out of school; he got kicked out. Never did a bit of work. I don't know why he was there in the first place. The only thing he seemed at all into was his part-time job at the Emerson Record World. But there was some problem there too. I have the feeling he got fired. Anyway, I stopped seeing him there when I went in to buy albums. Pretty soon after that, I stopped seeing him around campus at all."

"A record store, Ned?" Nancy asked, a funny feeling in the pit of her stomach. "Isn't it a little weird, all this record stuff?" Nancy watched Dave climb into the back of the limo. Then the thought hit like a cyclone. "Oh no, Ned!" Her voice was low. "He fits the exact description."

"What description? What are you saying?"

"I think Dave might have been one of the guys backstage the night Barton disappeared! He could even have been the one who hit me over the head. Maybe that's why he kept giving me such funny looks!"

Nancy darted from the club entrance into the

street, determined to make out the license plate before the limo vanished. But just as she passed a pile of crates, Ned cried, "Nancy, look out!" Nancy had never heard such panic in his voice. She turned suddenly, looking back at him, but lost her balance.

As she fell, her eyes caught the glint of something metallic cutting through the air and heading straight for her. Her body slammed onto the sidewalk as a knife jammed into a crate just inches away. It quivered there, giving its serpentine handle the illusion of movement.

Ned was by her side in seconds, but Nancy was already on her feet, running down the street as the limo pulled around a corner. "It stopped for a moment," she said, "as if they were waiting to see what would happen."

The limo was too far ahead to catch, but she did see the license plate. The numbers were caked with mud, but the decoration on the right side was clearly visible: a dragon with its tail curved into an L! Then it turned the corner and sped off into the night.

"Did you see the dragon?" Nancy asked breathlessly.

"Yeah, I saw it. Nancy, are you all right?"

"I guess so." She trembled at the thought of her near brush with death. "The fall didn't hurt much, but that knife came pretty close. Come on, let's get it. Someone has finally given us our first real clue!"

Cautiously they ran to the pile of crates where Nancy had fallen. "The police might be able to lift some—" She came to a sudden stop and stared in amazement at the crate. "It's gone! The knife is *gone!*"

Chapter Ten

"THEN WE FLAGGED a cab and tried to follow him, but he was too far ahead of us. We couldn't find him," Nancy told George, spearing a french fry and popping it into her mouth.

"So first thing this morning we called the manager of the Emerson Record World." Ned picked up where Nancy had left off. "It turns out that Dave Peck was fired for buying cheap pirated records. He charged the store the regular price, then deposited the extra money in his personal account! They got wise to what he was doing when one of the stockroom clerks discovered that the codes on the records were missing."

"You're kidding!" George put down her coffee

cup with a chink. "Wow! That sleazy guy could play a really important part in this mystery, huh?"

"You know it." Nancy finally felt she was on the trail that would crack this case. "I bet anything Dave's ring has a dragon on it," she went on, "and his ring and license plate match the wallet I found at the Music Hall. If the wallet belongs to Dave, maybe Ann Nordquist is in the clear."

"A good thing, since she and your dad are spending the day together," Ned remarked. "I think he really likes her."

"Hmm, I can't say I'm entirely comfortable with that," Nancy admitted. "And I won't be until I know what's going on."

George nodded. "Well, one way or the other, the truth will come out, as they say. So, anyhow, what'd you do next?"

"Well, the record store didn't know where to get in touch with him, so Ned called up the Emerson College registrar's office. His roommate works there a few hours a day, and Ned talked him into looking up Dave's mother's telephone number. The problem is she doesn't answer. We're going to try her again after breakfast."

George nodded. "Well, if there's anything I can do . . ."

"Thanks. I'll definitely let you know," Nancy said. "So, now that we've told you about the rest of our night, how was yours?"

"Pretty good. They played some really hot dancing music. But we didn't stay all that long after you guys left. Everyone was kind of keyed up about Barton. Roger especially."

"I can understand that," Nancy said. "What are he and the rest of the band going to do about tonight's performance if Barton's still a no show by concert time?"

"Alan," George said simply.

Nancy groaned. "I was afraid of that. You know, if Alan keeps getting to fill in on these gigs, he's never going to come clean with what he knows about Barton. I mean, why should he? As long as Barton's not around, Alan's a star."

"And is he playing the part," George added. "He took Bess over to the Hard Rock Cafe for a midnight supper after we left the club. He said all the biggest names in the music world hang out there. I think he was counting himself as one of them."

Nancy's expression grew dark. "I can't believe Bess. She's buying in to Alan's fantasy without stopping to consider how much harm he might be doing."

"So you really think Alan's hiding something? I mean, I know he's on another planet these days, but do you really think he'd put Barton's life in danger?"

"The only way to answer that question is to get to the bottom of whatever's going on," Nancy said. "Speaking of which, we'd better start calling Dave's mother again." She finished up her eggs and pushed her plate away. "Ready?" She stood up.

"Reporting for duty, Detective Drew," Ned replied, and the three friends stood up.

Several hours later, in the Drews' suite, they still were having no luck. Ned dialed Mrs. Peck's number for what seemed to Nancy like the thousandth time, and Nancy and George held their breath. "One ring," Ned announced. "Two. Three."

Nancy rolled her eyes in frustration.

"Hello? Is this Mrs. Peck?"

Ned began talking, and Nancy sat up straight and hung on to his every word.

"Mrs. Peck, my name is Ned Nickerson. I'm a—a friend of Dave's," Ned fibbed, looking slightly sheepish.

"We went to school together, Mrs. Peck," Ned went on. "Yes, as a matter of fact, I saw him just last night." Ned seemed relieved to be saying something truthful. "But he forgot to give me his address. That's why I'm calling, actually." Ned paused, his brow furrowed. "You don't?" He rolled his eyes. "If you'll excuse my saying so, that's—well, that's a little surprising to me."

"George," Nancy exclaimed. "How can a man's own mother not have his address? There is definitely something weird going on."

"Yes, I see," Ned said, signaling for quiet. "Then, do you know who his partner is? Oh, his boss—okay. His name is Lee? But you don't know how to contact him either?" Nancy's heart sank.

"Whew!" Ned sighed when he finally hung up the phone. "If I hadn't said I had to go, she would have gone on all day."

"So tell," Nancy demanded, a touch impatiently.

"Oh, sorry, Nan. Well, Dave's mother obviously thinks Dave's the greatest thing since sliced bread, even though she's disappointed he left school."

"But she doesn't know where he is half the time," Nancy put in.

"She told me his work takes him to so many places he can't have a permanent address. But she sure was quick to add that he calls her every week."

"To keep up the image of the perfect son," George observed.

"Except that he lives out of a suitcase," Nancy said. "All set to pick up and move if anyone's on his tail."

Ned agreed. "That business Dave's involved in can't be aboveboard. Anyway, his mother said his boss is a guy named Lee. James Lee. She started telling me how this Lee took her and 'her Davey' out to some restaurant in New York that Lee's brother owns. She would have told me what they had eaten, too, if I'd let her." He shook his head. "You know, I felt bad misleading her about Dave and me. She seemed kind of lonely."

"Poor woman. She probably deserves a lot better than Dave," Nancy said sympathetically. "When I get my hands on him . . ."

"But Nan, he doesn't have an address," George reminded her friend. "How are you going to find him?"

Nancy was silent for several minutes, contemplating. "Listen, Dave said he likes to keep up with the music scene, right?"

"Right," Ned affirmed.

"Well, isn't tonight's concert the most talked about show around? Bent Fender plays 'Rock for Relief' at the Rotunda," Nancy said, paraphrasing a radio advertisement, "the chic nightspot everyone wants to be seen at."

"Yeah, Roger was telling us last night that there will be huge crowds of people outside the Rotunda begging the doormen to let them pay their twenty-dollar admission charge and come inside," George injected. "Doesn't that sound nuts?"

"When you're hot, you're hot," Ned said, grinning. "But I see what you're getting at, Nancy. This is just the kind of scene a guy like Dave wouldn't miss."

"Exactly. So all we have to do is show up—and keep our fingers crossed that Dave will too."

* * *

"Wow! Look at all those people," Nancy exclaimed as she, Ned, and George arrived at the Rotunda later that evening. "How're they all going to fit inside?"

"A lot of them aren't," Ned replied. "That's part of the gimmick. If you keep a huge crowd of people standing outside your club, dying to get in, everyone will think it's popular, the place to be. And everyone who gets in will feel extra special about being there—you know, a member of the elite."

"Yuck. I'd have too much pride to stand out here praying the doormen would pick me out of the crowd." George wrinkled her nose in disgust.

"I'm with you," agreed Nancy. "It's a good thing we're on the guest list." They walked around to a lane cordoned off for guests of the club and people with free passes.

"You're on my list too," Ned whispered in Nancy's ear, his lips grazing her cheek.

Nancy almost melted. "And you're on mine," she said. Ned looked so handsome in his jeans and black pullover sweater. But despite her confident manner, Nancy still wondered about their relationship. The two of them needed time to relax together, time to really laugh and let loose and put their problems in the past, where they belonged. Until the mystery was solved, that would be impossible.

Once they were inside the club, Nancy's thoughts turned to Dave Peck. Determined to hunt him down, she and Ned split up and swept through the rooms of each of the three levels of the elegant club, searching every corner. Nancy was impressed by the vastness and extravagance.

The people were varied, from elegant to bizarre, exotic to all-American. Nancy looked at each one, her search for Dave dead-ending in an upstairs room that was lined with televisions all tuned to MTV. Ned was waiting for her there, and it was plain from his expression that he'd had no more luck than she had.

"No sign of him?" Nancy said.

Ned shook his head no.

"I saw a few people I knew, but not Dave. Vivian, Mr. Marshall's secretary, was down by the stage. And I saw Bess with Alan, not that she would talk to me." Nancy slumped down in an armchair and stared blankly at the checkerboard of television screens.

Ned sat down next to her. A heavy bass beat filled the room as a wild music video came to life on all the screens simultaneously.

The song faded, and a familiar Bent Fender tune came on. Nancy watched the screen a bit more attentively. The video cut from one scene to another, a collage of different shots. As Barton launched into the chorus of the song, a crowd scene came on, men and women emerging from a subway station. In the crowd were the members of Bent Fender themselves and several other people Nancy recognized. Linda Ferrare's cousin was there—the boy George had been dancing with the night before—and a woman who was the female lookalike of Mark Bailey, the guitarist. His sister, Nancy surmised.

Fender had chosen to use people they knew, rather than using actors to fill out the crowd. Nancy spotted Ann Nordquist, and her stomach did a nervous flip-flop. Her father and Ann were out again this evening.

But she forgot about them, her eyes suddenly glued to a television screen. Coming up the staircase on screen was a couple, kissing. The man was short. He had longish wavy brown hair and a familiar-looking, stocky, muscular physique. In amazement Nancy stepped up to the television screens.

"Ned, you won't believe this," she said slowly.

"What?"

"In a way . . . we did find Dave." Nancy pointed at the screen and at the same time tried to figure out who Dave was with. The girl's face was mostly hidden, but when the twosome reached the top of the staircase and pulled apart, Nancy let out a gasp. "I can't believe it! Ned, *look!* It's *Vivian!* What if she and Dave are a number off the screen as well as on!"

Instantly, Nancy was running. "Come on, Ned. Vivian was just downstairs. We have to find her."

Down the two flights of stairs Nancy flew, around the side of the dance floor and toward the stage where she had last seen Vivian. Ned was right behind her.

She scanned the mass of people, picking out the back of Vivian's jet-black coif. Marshall's secretary was in the wings to one side of the stage, talking to someone. The person leaned forward, into the light, and Nancy saw his scowling face. *Alan.* He moved his hands wildly, saying something Nancy couldn't hear.

Moving in closer, Nancy motioned to Ned to stay down below stage level where they wouldn't be seen. The dance music stopped. Linda Ferrare was tuning her bass. Mark Bailey was adjusting one of his guitar strings. A surge of excitement raced through the crowd as they waited for the band.

But Alan and Vivian continued to face off. "No!" Alan said furiously. Nancy and Ned were close enough now to make out what he was saying. "It's gotten totally out of control! I had no idea—"

"Save it, pest," Vivian interrupted. "You'll come around. I'm going to make absolutely sure of it."

"No way, Vivian. As soon as the concert is over, I'm going to tell Nancy everything.

"And what's more, I'm going to tell Bess too." Alan looked behind him. Nancy couldn't see through the dark curtain at the edge of the stage, but it was clear that Bess was back there, probably standing just out of earshot.

"But Alan," Vivian singsonged nastily, "if you tell Bess what you know, you'll have to admit that you lied about seeing Barton."

"I knew it!" Nancy exclaimed under her breath.

"Your precious angel won't like that one little bit," Vivian mocked.

"I can only hope she'll understand," Alan said. "I never should have believed your stories in the first place."

Nancy and Ned exchanged glances.

"The second I finish my last note, Vivian, you're through." Nancy could hear Alan's footsteps as he stormed away and took his place on stage.

"Don't count on it!" Vivian called out, her voice following him, and she let out a frightening laugh.

"What do you suppose she means by that?" Ned asked.

"I don't know, but I don't like the sound of it."

Nancy and Ned made their way to a table when they were out of Vivian's field of vision. By then the band had assembled on stage, their instruments fully tuned, their sound levels set.

Alan was watching Jim Parker, seated behind his keyboard console. Jim gave an almost imperceptible nod, and the band let their first chords wail.

They were halfway into their second number when Alan's amp began crackling with ear-piercing static. He stopped playing immediately and fiddled with some dials on the equipment. Suddenly, sparks spewed from one of the wires. Someone in the audience screamed. Then the equipment went dead—and the club was plunged into total darkness!

Chapter Eleven

"WHAT'S HAPPENING?" A girl shrieked. "Is it a hold-up or something?"

"No," someone else shouted. "It's a fire!"

"Fire?" a man yelled fearfully.

Mass confusion broke loose.

Separated from Ned, Nancy was jostled from two sides as she inched in what she hoped was the direction of the closest wall. She waved her arms in front of her until her hands found the smooth, solid plaster. Turning, she pressed her back to it, squeezing out of the way of the hordes of people making blind, panicked dashes in every direction.

"Simon? Simon, where are you?" a woman

near Nancy was screaming, her voice filled with terror. "Simon, are you all right?"

"Stay calm!" Nancy called out to her. "The lights will be back on in a few minutes."

"Simon!" the woman kept shrieking.

"Ladies and gentlemen, please do not panic." A new voice filled the air, loud and hollow. Someone was speaking through a megaphone. "The electrical short on stage caused a temporary power outage, but the electricity should be restored in a matter of minutes. Please stay where you are. I repeat, stay where you are."

Nancy eased herself into a sitting position on the floor to wait. She could hear others do the same. But as the panic subsided, her own fears began to blossom in the overwhelming blackness. Had the power outage been an accident? Or was it perhaps a little too convenient, coming as it did on the heels of Vivian's threat to Alan?

The minutes ticked away. Nancy prayed to herself that this would be no rerun of the night Barton disappeared. Then, suddenly, the power came flooding back on. Nancy blinked, needing to adjust her eyes even to the subdued lighting of the club. The band stood on stage, checking their instruments and amplifiers now that the electricity was working again. But one person was missing. Where was Alan?

Nancy felt panic rising in her throat. Then she noticed that the curtain shielding the backstage area from the audience had been pulled down, a casualty of the frenzied rush of people immediately following the blackout. She let out a noisy sigh of relief as she saw Alan standing off to one side, staring at a sheet of paper.

Ned was still more or less where he had been before the power had blown. As he looked around, Nancy waved to him. He caught sight of her, his face softening with relief, and made his way across the room. Nancy kissed him quickly.

"Listen, Ned," she said. "I'm going to go talk to Alan and see what he wanted to tell me. Maybe you should go look for George and make sure she's okay."

"What about Bess?" Ned wanted to know. "I don't see her back there." He looked behind the stage.

"I'll ask Alan about her."

"Meet you back here?" Ned asked.

"In ten minutes." Nancy hoisted herself onto the stage and headed straight for Alan. She wasn't bothered by any guards. They were trying to restore order in the club. The concert evening was over.

Alan stood rooted to the stage floor. He was staring blankly ahead of him, his cheeks pale, his eyes glazed. His right hand shook violently as he clutched his guitar.

"Hey," Nancy called out gently. "Alan."

He whipped his head around in her direction. "What?" he said, his voice as tight as a rubber band at the point of snapping.

"What's wrong?" Nancy moved to his side and touched his arm. The hollow look in his eyes made her almost afraid to hear his answer.

"Wrong? Why should anything be wrong?"

"I heard you arguing with Vivian."

Alan inhaled sharply but said nothing.

"I know you didn't really see Barton," Nancy prodded, "so why don't you tell me the rest?"

Alan shook his head back and forth, never lifting his eyes to meet Nancy's. "No. No, I can't. You wouldn't understand." Nancy sensed the terror behind the stubborn words.

"How am I supposed to understand if you don't tell me?" she asked. Only a short time before he had seemed so determined to let her in on whatever he knew. What horrible thing had happened while the lights were out to make him change his mind so completely?

"Alan," Nancy persisted, "that blackout happened for a reason, didn't it?"

"Please," Alan begged, "I said I'm not talking."

"Okay. I can't force you. But at least tell me where Bess is. I thought she was back here."

Alan bit down hard on his lower lip, and Nancy could see it tremble.

"Oh, *Alan!*" Nancy cried. "It isn't Bess, is it?" She held her breath. Alan didn't utter a sound. "Alan!"

"She's fine," he whispered hoarsely. "Bess is fine."

"Where is she?" Nancy felt like a five-gear car being forced to run in first.

"She's sick. She went back to the hotel."

"Alone?"

"She took a taxi."

"How'd she get out of here so fast? The lights just came back on. Besides, I saw her when I got here, and she looked fine." Nancy reached for Alan's shoulders and started shaking him. "What's wrong with her? Tell me!"

"Hey, give me a break," he protested weakly, stepping back. "She left by the back door—had a cold or the flu or something, and she specifically asked that no one disturb her later tonight." Nancy listened to Alan's story gain momentum. "She went back to the hotel to take some cold medicine and go to sleep, okay? Are you finished giving me the third degree?"

Nancy let her arms drop. "You mean Bess went home to take her Motocillan?"

"Motocillan. That's right."

"Are you sure?"

"Of course I'm sure."

Nancy shivered, despite the warm air inside the club. "Alan," she said coldly, "if Bess ever took Motocillan, she could die. She's allergic to it. Now tell me the truth."

The guitar slid out of Alan's hand. His knees gave out, and he slumped to the floor.

"I can't. I can't. If I tell they'll . . ."

"Who's they?" Nancy fought to stay calm. "Is

there anyone here you're afraid of?" She motioned to the members of Bent Fender, who had gathered around nervously when they'd seen Alan collapse.

Alan shook his head.

"Then how is anyone going to know you told us?" Nancy asked softly.

"Because you'll try to find her . . ."

"Bess? Then she's not back at the hotel." Nancy's voice hardened. "Alan, what's going on?"

Alan's words came out in a jumbled rush. "You can't go after her—the shipment—they'll hurt her if the shipment doesn't go out tonight. Please, just let them get it out . . ."

"What shipment? Alan, I swear, I'd never do anything to harm Bess. You've got to believe me."

Alan sighed deeply. "They grabbed her," he rasped, "during the blackout so I wouldn't tell you what I heard. I don't know where they took her."

"Who's they? Vivian? Mr. Marshall?"

"Marshall?" Puzzled, Alan looked up. "No, not him."

"You mean Vivian's in on this, but Harold Marshall isn't?"

"That witch," Alan said through clenched teeth. "Everyone thinks Marshall is the boss, but Vivian's got him running around in circles, and he's too stupid and egotistical to realize it. He's like a marionette, and she's pulling all the strings."

"Of course!" Nancy nodded grimly. "How could we have been so blind? Roger, remember you said Vivian would do anything for Marshall? She buttered him up until she had complete control over him. Marshall's huge ego made him take credit for all the ideas she fed him, which was exactly what Vivian wanted. That way, if anyone caught on to what she was doing, her boss would shoulder the blame. I almost fell for it too."

"It's an easy mistake to make," Roger said. "Marshall's personality doesn't exactly make you want to give him the benefit of the doubt." His mouth settled into a tight line. "Although he did offer you that record contract, didn't he?" Roger turned to Alan.

Alan hesitated.

"You promise that nothing will happen to Bess if I tell you?" Alan asked again.

"Alan, we're all Bess's friends," Nancy assured him. "I know she and I had that fight, but I love Bess. If anything happens to her—"

"Okay. You were right to think that Marshall offered me the contract just to get me to tell you I'd seen Barton. But I didn't think about that, just like I didn't realize that Marshall's offer was *Vivian's* idea. I didn't see anything I didn't want to see. I was so wrapped up in the idea of being famous . . ." Alan pounded his fist against the floor. "This whole thing is my fault. If I hadn't been so convinced I was star material, Bess would be safe right now."

"Alan, this is no time to start blaming yourself," Nancy said firmly. "You have to tell us what you know so we can figure out what to do about it."

"I really believed them. I thought they wanted me to record because they thought I was good. And when Marshall told me that Barton's disappearance was a publicity stunt, I believed that, too. I mean, I *wanted* to believe it. As long as he was all right, but out of the picture, he was my ticket to success. So when Harold Marshall asked me to tell you I saw Barton, I agreed. Don't get me wrong. I really believed Barton was fine."

"But Alan, I thought you said Marshall didn't have anything to do with whatever is going on," said Nancy, confused.

"That's right. He didn't. Vivian planted the publicity idea in his head and then told him she'd take care of the details. So when you started asking questions, Nancy, he thought you were nosing in where you didn't belong. Vivian convinced him to offer me a contract in exchange for getting you off his back. Of course, neither of them ever expected to let me go through with the recording." Alan toyed with a strand of dark curly hair. "I guess I was a fool."

"Alan," Nancy asked impatiently, "how do you know all this?"

"I'm getting to that. See, I had convinced myself that my lie about Barton wouldn't hurt anyone, but when you and Bess had that fight, I saw that something was wrong. To make things worse, Bess was defending me when I didn't even deserve it."

"Why didn't you level with her right then and there? And with me?" Nancy bent down to look Alan in the eye.

"I wanted to. But I was so afraid Bess would hate me for it. I just didn't have the guts to confess." Regret was etched on his face, and Nancy felt her anger toward him soften a bit.

"So I stuck to my lie," Alan went on, "but I just didn't feel right about it after that. You started me worrying about whether Barton really was all right, and I realized that if anything happened to him, it would be partially my fault. I still couldn't bring myself to tell Bess then, but I decided that, at the very least, I ought to go to Mr. Marshall and insist that I see Barton in person. Just to know for sure." Alan took a breath.

"Anyhow, I went over to his office late this afternoon, while Bess was out jogging. He wasn't there, but Vivian was. She was sitting in his office using the telephone, and the door was open a crack. I could hear everything she said, and it was what I just told you about the publicity story and my record contract."

"And something about a shipment of some sort?" Nancy asked, recalling his earlier words.

"Yeah. I don't know what kind of shipment, but she told whoever she was talking to that it was going out tonight."

"The bootleg albums," Nancy said. "Did she say where they were being shipped to?"

"Heading east, that's all."

"Weird," Roger said. "I thought New York was as far east as you could get. Maybe she meant the east side of town."

"Or maybe she wasn't talking about this country at all," Nancy said. "Maybe by east she meant the eastern hemisphere."

"Like China?" Roger asked.

"Exactly," Nancy sighed. Her hunch about the lack of copyright laws in that country could very well play out. But that didn't make her feel any better. It meant that Ann Nordquist might not be off the hook after all.

However, any further thoughts about China and Ann Nordquist ceased when Alan began talking again. "I don't know if the destination is going to matter much when you hear the rest of Vivian's conversation," he said.

"Oh no." Nancy steeled herself for what was next.

"Vivian said that there was a body going out with the shipment."

"Barton!" Roger Gold exclaimed in horror.

"Tell me Vivian's exact words," Nancy instructed Alan, her heart filling with dread.

Alan tensed. "Like I said, 'one body going out with the shipment,' was the way she put it. Then the person on the other end of the phone must have said something. Vivian answered, 'No, we're going to do it right before we ship him out—silence him for good.'" Alan's voice was shaking again. "The last thing I heard was, 'Yeah, pick up at the duck house, as usual. Ten-thirty. Right.' Then Vivian hung up."

Nancy glanced at her watch. Nine o'clock. "What happened next?" she said, her own voice trembling. If she couldn't find Barton in an hour and a half, she might never find him—*alive*—or find Bess either!

"I tried to sneak out," Alan said, "but I was so freaked out about what I'd overheard that I knocked something over as I was leaving the outer office—a chair, I think. After that, I just ran as fast as I could, down the stairs and out the building. I went to the hotel and got Bess and brought her here to the club. I thought I got away clean."

"But you didn't tell Bess what you'd heard?" Nancy asked.

Alan shook his head. "I knew I had to tell you everything—tonight, I thought, here at the club—so I figured I'd level with Bess at the same time. Besides, I guess I wanted to put that part off as long as possible, having Bess find out she'd fallen for a worthless bum."

"But how did Vivian find out you knew?" Nancy asked.

Alan reddened. "Vivian looked out the window and saw me leaving. She knew she'd find me here at the concert."

"So she arranged the power outage and had Bess kidnapped to keep you from talking?" Nancy asked, beginning to put all the pieces together.

Alan stood up, reached into the back pocket of his leather pants, and pulled out a crinkled piece of yellow lined paper. Silently, he handed it to Nancy.

She smoothed it out and read the words printed in bold, box letters. *DO NOT SAY A WORD TO ANYONE IF YOU WANT TO SEE YOUR GIRLFRIEND AGAIN,* the note read.

Chapter Twelve

"WHO GAVE THIS to you?" Nancy demanded, waving the note.

"Someone pulled me off stage and pressed it into my hand while the lights were out," Alan explained.

"What I don't get is why they didn't just take Alan." Roger said.

"I think they realized that if Alan vanished before this show, like Barton did before the last one, it was going to look pretty suspicious. And they wouldn't have such an easy time explaining it the second time around."

"I wish they *had* taken me," Alan said. "I

didn't mean for anyone to get hurt. I was so busy dreaming about how famous I'd be. If anything happens to Bess—or Barton—"

"We've got to find out where they're shipping from," Nancy put in, "and get there fast!"

"But you can't look for her!" Alan's voice rang out. "You promised. If they realize you're coming after them, who knows what they'll do to Bess!"

"Alan, think about it," Nancy said, barely able to face the facts herself. "We don't have any choice. You heard Vivian's plans for Barton. If we don't go after them, there may be two bodies going out with the albums."

"What are we going to do?" Anguish was written all over Alan's face.

"We're going to get ourselves out of this madness out here," Nancy said, determined. "And then we're going to find that duck house Vivian mentioned."

A few moments later, Nancy was running her index finger down the listings in a telephone book. "Duck House. Let's see. D-U-B, D-U-C . . . Duck. The Duck's Back, Duck Floor Coverings, Duck Sport and Leisure Shop. No Duck House." She slammed the heavy book shut. "Any luck, George?"

George shook her head. She was bent over the yellow pages. "No pet stores with that name. Maybe duck house isn't the *name* of the place, just a place that has duck."

"How about stores that specialize in aquariums and water habitats?" Alan suggested.

"You'd be more likely to find goldfish there," Nancy said.

"There are tons of pet stores listed that specialize in birds," George said. "Not that we'd have any idea which ones to go to first."

"Maybe we should divide up," Roger Gold suggested. "There are enough of us to cover a pretty big area."

With the concert postponed, the members of Bent Fender had gathered with Nancy, Alan, Ned, and George in the private office of the club manager, to try to come up with a rescue plan.

"Well, it's true, there are plenty of us," Nancy said, "but if we split up, I don't see how one or two of us is going to be much of a match for a gang of killers. Besides, like George said, who knows if 'the duck house' has anything to do with pet shops at all? It's just a shot in the dark."

"But it's the only shot we've come up with so far," Alan reminded her anxiously. "Listen, there's 'Jungle Paradise,' 'Birds of a Feather,' 'Hot House Exotic Birds' . . ."

"Somehow, I don't exactly think a duck is considered an exotic bird." Nancy's mouth settled into a grim line.

"Or even a pet, really." Linda Ferrare spoke up.

"The truth is, I kind of think of it as something to eat. You know, like Peking duck," Roger Gold put in. "What a time to be thinking about food," he said with a rueful smile.

"Roger!" Nancy jumped out of the lounge chair she had been sitting in. "Say that again."

"What? What a time to be thinking about food?"

"No, before that."

"Peking duck?"

"That's it! Why didn't I think of it right away?"

Ned put a hand on Nancy's shoulder. "You want to let the rest of us in on it, Nan?"

"The Duck House, the lack of copyright laws in Mainland China, James Lee." Nancy reeled off a list of clues.

"James Lee. You mean Dave Peck's boss?" Ned asked. "I still don't get it."

"Don't you see? Mrs. Peck said James Lee's brother had taken her and Dave to a restaurant his brother owned, right? What if 'Lee' is the Chinese last name. It could even be 'Li.' Remember, we've never seen it spelled."

"You mean Dave's boss might be the connection to China. And Ann Nordquist isn't mixed up in all of this?" Ned asked.

"Exactly," Nancy affirmed. "China just might be his native country, and the place where he still has black-market contacts." She grabbed the yellow pages and thumbed through them. "All right! Roger, you did it! You hit the nail on the head! Here it is! Li's Duck House in Chinatown!" She clapped triumphantly. "Bess and Barton, here we come!"

Nancy got out of the cab that had sped her to the restaurant. Ned, George, and Alan got out too. Another taxi behind them dropped off Roger, Linda, Jim, and Mark.

Across the street was a four-story building. The windows of the top two floors were boarded up. The two lower floors were bright with lighted windows, through which Nancy could see diners seated at tables laden with tureens and platters of food. A deep red facade decorated the lower level, with a sign above the entrance spelling out "Li's Duck House." Sure enough, the L of Li's was formed from the tail of an ornate dragon.

"That cinches it!" Nancy announced, pointing to the sign. "That L on the dragon, it must be a sort of calling card for Li and everybody who works for him. I'm sure the limo Dave was in belongs to him, too."

She strode toward the curb. But Ned followed and caught hold of her arm. "Nan, the people who have Bess and Barton aren't playing games. Don't you think we should wait for the police to get here? Sergeant Wald said—"

Nancy had telephoned the police just before leaving the club and arranged for them to meet her at Li's Duck House. She could still hear Sergeant Wald's words ringing in her ears. "The Li gang is involved in everything from gambling to smuggling. Watch out, kid. They're dangerous."

"No," Nancy answered firmly. "We have to get Bess and Barton out of there! The sergeant and his officers will be our backup."

"But we can't very well waltz into that restaurant and ask them to turn Bess and Barton over," George said sensibly.

"That's why the rest of you are going to wait here while I go scout out the building."

"Nancy," Ned said sternly, "remember what you said earlier. If it comes down to one of us against a whole gang of them, it won't be much of a match."

"It won't come down to that."

"At least let me come with you," Alan spoke up. "I was the one who got us into this mess, at least in part, so let me help you get us out."

"Well, okay. Maybe it would be safer for two of us to go in."

Once inside the restaurant, Nancy breathed in the warm, spicy-smelling odor, then gave a quick but thorough look around. Most of the dozen tables were occupied by diners. In the rear, the kitchen was partially visible through the windows of swinging metal doors. To one side was a flight of stairs going up and another flight going down. A sign for the restrooms and telephones hung over an arrow pointing downstairs.

"Two for dinner?" A woman approached Nancy and Alan, holding out menus.

"Oh, ah, would you mind if I used your restroom?" Nancy asked politely.

The woman frowned. "Customers only," she said coldly.

"My uncle eats here every week," Nancy lied. Her blood was running cold, but she flashed her warmest smile. "A tall man, gray hair and a mustache. I was here with him just last Sunday."

The woman stood aside. "All right," she said grudgingly, "go ahead."

Nancy glanced at the clock located over the metal swinging doors. It was already a quarter to ten, and she had only until ten-thirty to find Bess. That left only forty-five minutes—and time was running out fast!

Chapter Thirteen

THE HOSTESS TURNED away, and Nancy tugged at Alan's sleeve. "We've got to hurry! When no one's looking, go up to the next floor and see what you can find. Look for another staircase. I'm going to check out the downstairs, but so many people have access to it, I think the top floors are our best bet."

Alan grabbed Nancy's hand and squeezed it warmly. When the coast was clear, he headed for the stairs.

In the basement, Nancy found an open space with two wall telephones and a shabby sofa. Off this area were two tiny restrooms and a closed door. The door opened easily. Behind it was a large boiler, water pipes, a central heating unit, old kitchenware, and a walk-in refrigerator. Wall shelves were lined with cans of Chinese ingredients. But there was no sign of either the two prisoners or a shipment of records.

Nancy raced back up the steps. Then, unnoticed, she went up the next flight. She found Alan standing at the edge of the second-floor dining room. "No luck" was the meaning of the look they gave each other.

Waiters were carrying food to the customers from a dumbwaiter that was positioned on one wall. The staircase Nancy had come up ended there, and she saw no exits that could have led to the third floor. She surveyed the ceiling, looking for a trap door.

Nothing.

Alan gave her a helpless shrug. "Maybe people going upstairs use *that.*" He pointed to a dumbwaiter, half-concealed by a partition.

Nancy gave him a look. "I suppose, if you're prepared to tie yourself up like a pretzel."

"Sorry. It was a dumb suggestion." Alan sighed. "But how else do you get to those top floors?"

"There's got to be a way. They can't possibly move heavy loads of record albums down on a dumbwaiter." *Not to mention moving down a body—or two bodies.*

Don't think of Barton and Bess as "bodies,"

Nancy scolded herself, but she sensed Alan was thinking the same thing. She glanced at her watch. It was coming on to ten o'clock, scarcely more than half an hour before pickup. If nothing had gone wrong, Bess and Barton were alive and somewhere in the building. But where?

Nancy looked around once more at the people enjoying their dinners under a tapestry depicting a serene waterfall. It hurt her to watch life going on as usual while Bess's and Barton's lives were still at stake.

The tapestry! Suddenly Nancy realized what she'd missed on her first look around the room. "Follow me," she whispered urgently to Alan. She moved toward the tapestry, which decorated the wall opposite the windows she'd seen when she'd gotten out of the taxi. As she and Alan crossed the room she discreetly put a hand to her left ear and removed one of her blue teardrop earrings, which she then dropped into her shirt pocket.

"Excuse me," she said to a couple at one of the tables beneath the woven wall hanging, then gestured toward Alan. "My friend and I had dinner at this table earlier in the evening, and I think I might have dropped an earring. Do you mind if I take a look?"

"Go right ahead," said a silver-haired man, getting up from his chair to allow Nancy to look behind the table.

Quickly, she bent down and grasped one of the bottom corners of the tapestry. When she lifted it up, she saw a window. That was it! The rear of the building faced the next street. There was probably a second entrance at the back. All she had to do was go around to the next block to find the door to the top two floors.

"What are you doing?" the man asked. "How could your earring possibly get behind the tapestry?"

"I'm sorry. No time to explain." Nancy took Alan's arm and tore down the stairs and out of the building, leaving the man to stare after them.

The plain brown truck sat outside the other side of the building, the cab doors open. "All ready to load in the albums," George hissed to Nancy as she and the others peered around the corner of the block.

"Not just the albums," Nancy said with grave apprehension. "We can't wait for the police any longer. We've got to move in right now."

"But what about that heavyset man at the door?" Roger said. "He might be armed."

At that moment, the guard stubbed out the end of the cigarette he'd been smoking and pulled open the door he had been standing in front of. A short man in dark clothes came out carrying a large crate.

"Dave!" Nancy whispered. "With a load of albums!"

"But they're early. They weren't supposed to start until ten-thirty," Alan said.

"I know," Nancy replied grimly. "We've got even less time than we thought. Where on earth is Sergeant Wald? When Dave brings down the last box, Bess and Barton are through." Dave put the crate into the truck. Behind him, a taller heavyset man came out with another crate, and then a third man emerged. The tall man fit the description the Radio City Music Hall guards had given of the man who had been Dave's partner.

"Okay, guys, listen up," Nancy said, gathering everyone around. "We have to put Dave and his pals out of commission for a while. There are more of us than them, so if we take them by surprise, it shouldn't be too tough. Once we're inside, we'll break into groups to look for Bess and Barton."

"What if more of those creeps are inside?" Mark Bailey asked.

"Then we'd better pray their hands are full of crates and that we're faster than they are," Nancy replied uneasily. "Now, I'm going to go ask Mr. Muscles over there for a cigarette." She pointed toward the guard. "While he's holding the match for me, I'm going to practice a new move we learned in karate."

Nancy rounded the corner, walking slowly toward the guarded door.

The guard watched Nancy's progress down the

narrow, empty side street. He shifted uneasily when she made eye contact and gave him a tentative smile.

"Can you spare a smoke?" she asked, hoping her voice sounded normal.

Arching a bushy eyebrow, the guard looked down the block, which was home to a handful of grocery stores that were closed for the night. Then he put a hand into his jacket pocket and pulled out a red and white box. After giving Nancy a cigarette, he fished around in another pocket for a book of matches.

Nancy was close enough to make out the L-tailed dragon on the matchbook. James Li again. She put the cigarette in her mouth. The guard held a lit match with one hand, cupping the other around the flame as Nancy bent forward and edged the tip of the cigarette toward the light. Then, in one brisk, split-second movement, she smashed the heel of her hand into the guard's chin. He didn't even have a chance to shout before he fell to the pavement.

"Ned, Roger," she called out. "Quick. Give me a hand." They hoisted the unconscious guard into the back of the truck. Then they waited behind the door to the building. When Dave and his cohorts reappeared, they jumped them.

Dave fought free from the surprise attack. Nancy brought her right arm up for a blow, but he caught hold and pinned it behind her back, twisting painfully. By then, though, the others had appeared. George and Alan helped Nancy overpower Dave, while Linda, Mark, and Jim gave Roger and Ned a hand in carrying the other two, still kicking and fighting, into the back of the truck.

They finally shoved Dave in too and slammed the back door shut. With her left arm, Nancy snapped closed several padlocks that were attached to it, imprisoning the four men in their own vehicle. "There. That ought to hold them for a while." Nancy allowed herself a second to inspect her twisted right shoulder. She could hardly lift her arm, and she massaged the soreness with her other hand.

"Nancy, you're hurt!" George observed anxiously.

"It's not that bad." Nancy said, steeling herself against the pain.

"Are you sure?"

Nancy managed a stiff smile in spite of the throbbing in her shoulder. "Okay," she said, "someone better wait down here for the police while we go in. Alan, will you volunteer?"

"I'll do whatever you say."

"Good. If you have any trouble, yell. The rest of you, follow me."

Inside, they groped their way up two dark, narrow flights of stairs and then split up, Ned and George exploring the third floor with Nancy, the musicians taking the top level.

"What a place to get stuck in without a flashlight," George muttered as their group inched forward blindly.

With Ned and George behind her, Nancy guided herself along the wall of what apparently was a narrow hallway. Suddenly her hand slid around a corner. The hallway had ended. "I think we're in a big room," Nancy whispered. "There's got to be a light switch somewhere near here."

"Pay dirt!" came Ned's voice, as fluorescent overhead lamps illuminated a huge loft space.

"Wow!" Nancy looked around her in amazement. The loft was filled with the best, most modern recording equipment available.

"Nancy! Ned! George!" It was Roger calling from above them down the staircase. "We found them! Hurry!"

The recording equipment forgotten, the three friends followed Roger's voice, racing upstairs and through another loft littered with cartons like the ones Dave and his cohorts had been carrying.

"In here!" Roger peered out from a smaller room partitioned off at the very back of the loft.

"Nancy!" cried Bess as Linda, Mark, and Jim finished untying the ropes that had bound her and Barton. "George! Ned!" Bess was on her feet, hugging them all at once. "I can't believe you found us! I thought I was never going to see any of you again!"

Nancy pulled Bess close with her left arm,

warm tears of relief trickling down both friends' cheeks. Nancy squeezed her as hard as she could. "Oh, Bess, thank heavens we got here in time!"

"I'll say," Barton Novak agreed tremulously. The members of Bent Fender were having their own reunion.

"Barton, are you okay? Did they hurt you?" Linda asked.

"Well, spending two days tied to a chair isn't my idea of a vacation." Barton grinned.

Bess was less ready to laugh off their near brush with death. "Oh, Nan, to think I didn't believe a single word you told me," she cried. "Barton was in this awful place, just like you said, and they were going to kill us . . ." Her sentence dissolved into sobs.

"It's okay, Bess," Nancy consoled her. "Everything's going to be fine."

"No it's not. I was so rotten to you. How can you ever forgive me. I apologize a million, trillion times."

"Hey, no need."

"Boy, just wait until I get my hands on that double-crossing liar Alan Wales."

"Wait a minute, Bess," Nancy said, surprising herself. "Don't be so hard on the guy. His biggest crime was just being swept away by his dreams."

"I don't know, Nancy. Those dreams almost got Barton and me murdered!" Bess paused. "So where is the rat, anyway?"

"Downstairs waiting for the police."

"You're very much mistaken," an unfamiliar male voice boomed out behind Nancy. "The police are downstairs in the basement, locked to the pipes with their own handcuffs."

Nancy whirled around to see a small man dressed in a neat gray suit, with a dark hat pulled low over his face. He held a gun. And the gun was pointed directly at Nancy!

The man smiled a bone-chilling, evil smile. "James Li at your service," he announced. "The next person who moves is dead."

Chapter Fourteen

"May I extend my congratulations, Miss Drew? You almost put a damper on my little party. Almost, but not quite." James Li gave a demonic laugh. "It is Miss Drew, isn't it?" He touched the tip of her nose with the cold, hard barrel of his gun.

The tap of high-heeled shoes sounded on the bare floor behind James Li. "That's Nancy Drew all right." Vivian stepped out of the shadows, Dave by her side. "This'll teach you to go poking around in business that doesn't concern you," she said.

Nancy remained silent, not giving Vivian the satisfaction of an answer.

"It's a pity my little warning the other night failed to scare you off," Li offered.

"That knife-throwing act was yours?" Nancy asked, an edge of bitterness to her voice.

"Through one of my boys."

"Lucky for me he missed."

"Lucky, Miss Drew? I told you it was just a warning. Otherwise . . ." The look in James Li's cold dark eyes more than finished the sentence. Nancy knew this man played for keeps. "Alas, it seems only the inevitable was delayed." Li smiled. "Did you really think you could stop us? I knew something was wrong tonight as soon as I saw your budding rock-and-roll star standing at the entrance instead of my guard, Petey. When Vivian told me who the young man was, we realized you must have traced us here. But no matter. I let my boys out of the truck, they told us the police were on their way, and we simply waited inside the entrance for your friend Sergeant Wald and his brave men in blue."

"But what did you do to Alan?" Bess demanded. "Not that I really care," she added unconvincingly.

James Li frowned. "A minor setback. He managed to get away while we were attending to the officers. But some of my boys went after him. He won't get far. As for the rest of you, I'll give you a chance to say your goodbyes to each other."

"How nice of you," muttered George.

"Once the truck is loaded," Li continued, "we're going to send you on a one-way trip."

Bess let out a choked cry.

"Don't worry, he won't get away with this," Nancy said.

"I wouldn't place any bets on that, Miss Drew. Dave, tie them up."

One by one, Dave pushed the prisoners down into hard, straight-back chairs, bound their wrists and ankles, and secured them to the chairs with more rope. He saved Nancy for last, pulling the rope extra tight. A shooting pain seared through her injured arm.

"That's for practicing your karate moves on me," he said, sneering.

"It evens the score," Nancy said through gritted teeth, "for that rap on the head at the concert. You were the one who hit me, weren't you, Dave?" She tried to keep a hard look on her face in spite of the burning pain in her shoulder. Ned also eyed Dave angrily. If he got the chance, he'd pay Dave back for hurting Nancy.

Nancy could hear the sounds of boxes being carried down the stairs. It was as if the boxes were sand in an hourglass. When the boxes were gone, it would be all over.

Li fired off more orders. "Okay, Dave, you help the boys finish loading up. Vivian, you take this gun and keep it pointed at our guests. If they so much as breathe too loudly, let them have it.

I'm going down to the ship to tell them to start the motors."

"The ship that's going to carry the records?" Nancy asked.

"And Vivian and my boys and me." James Li smiled. "There isn't a thing you can do to stop us. I'm not thrilled about leaving the States, but once Mr. Novak here caught on to what we were doing, things got a little too hot to handle. I decided to make one more big shipment and then leave the country until things cooled off. It was unfortunate that I had to wait until tonight before doing away with him, but I couldn't risk having his body found before I was safely aboard ship."

"Then Alan found out about your plans right before the final shipment," Nancy said. "But you were afraid the disappearance of a second Fender guitarist would attract too much attention right before the critical night."

"Very perceptive of you, Miss Drew. We didn't want the police alerted."

"But we were able to coax the story out of Alan . . . and contact the police. You didn't count on that."

"No," Li agreed. "But it didn't pose much of a problem in the end, did it?" His mouth spread in a frightening smile. "And now, ladies and gentlemen, it's time for me to say good night." He tipped his hat. "Dave, you know what to do once the truck is loaded." He looked back at Nancy. "You see, there's going to be a tragic fire in this warehouse. But then, I'm sure my brother won't mind collecting insurance on the building while we're out of the country, lying low. And the diners downstairs will certainly leave at the first sign of smoke. It's just a shame you people on the upper floor will be trapped." Li laughed cruelly. "All right, go ahead, Dave. I'll meet you at the ship when you're through."

"You're leaving *now?"* Confusion registered on Dave's face. "But we had a deal. I'd take care of the records. You'd take care of the people."

"Correct. That was our arrangement. But I'm changing the deal. I don't like dirty work, and I want to be far away while it's being done. Do you understand?"

"But boss, I can't. I've never . . . I mean, I know this guy." Dave pointed to Ned, horrified as he realized what Li expected him to do. "He was my friend, kind of."

"Dave, I am going down to the dock. We'll be pulling anchor in twenty minutes, record albums or no record albums. The police will be looking for their men as soon as they discover they're missing. If you want to stay around and visit the prison wards, fine. If you want passage on my ship for yourself and your girlfriend," he looked at Vivian, "you'd better do as I say." James Li turned on his heel. But heading out the door, he was intercepted by Petey, the guard Nancy had asked for the light.

"Hey, boss?" Petey said. "We got a problem. It's that kid. We looked everywhere for him. I don't know how he got away so quick. It's like he just vanished or something."

Li tapped his pistol nervously against his palm. "Well then, you'd better hurry with those albums. He might get to the cops."

Petey nodded.

"You too, Dave," Li commanded. "Get to work."

"But—"

"That's the end of the discussion." Li headed out.

Dave looked around at Nancy and the others. "Viv, what do you think?"

"You mean about them? I think we better do what Li says," Vivian told him. "I don't have any intention of winding up in jail."

"I guess." Dave handed her his gun (with some reluctance, Nancy thought), and went into the next room to move the crates of albums.

"Vivian, you're not really going to listen to James Li, are you?" With her hands tied behind her back, Nancy had no option other than to try to talk Vivian out of the drastic plan. She suspected that Vivian was the person to convince. Dave was clearly shaken up at the thought of being responsible for so much bloodshed. If

Vivian changed her mind, Nancy was certain that Dave would go along with her. "You wouldn't really set that fire," Nancy said.

"A lot you know," Vivian replied roughly. "Before Dave introduced me to Jimmy Li, every nickel I earned from my lousy job went toward the rent on a one-room dump. I never had fancy clothes or went to nice restaurants or owned real jewelry."

"And now you have it all?"

"These aren't rhinestones on my finger, sweetheart." Vivian flashed a sparkling ring of gold and diamonds.

"But are all those luxuries worth having murder on your conscience for the rest of your life? Think about it. We're talking about human lives."

"I know what we're talking about." Vivian's voice was deadly cold.

"Look, it's no longer just a question of stealing masters or illegally copying albums or even knocking me out backstage at the Music Hall," Nancy said desperately. "You must be pretty loyal to James Li to kill for him."

"He takes good care of Dave and me."

"Vivian, how long have you known him?"

"Dave introduced me to him a few months ago, when he needed to get on the inside at World Communications. But I don't see what difference that makes."

"And Dave hasn't worked for him very long, either."

"They started doing business when Dave worked at Emerson Record World."

"That was less than a year ago," Ned put in.

"And you're ready to put yourself entirely in the hands of someone you've known for such a short time?" Nancy asked. "A man who makes deals and then 'changes' them as it suits him? Vivian, you and Dave are planning on escaping to a country where you don't know a soul except Mr. Li. You don't speak the language, you don't know any of the customs. Without that man, you're lost. And he's ready to let you carry out murder, so that he isn't responsible for it."

Vivian seemed to be considering Nancy's words. But then her face hardened. "You don't really care what happens to Dave and me. You're just pleading for your own lives. Well, you all deserve exactly what you get. We had a great thing going, and you came along and messed it up."

Dave poked his head into the room. "We're about to bring the last load down."

Nancy drew in a sharp, frightened breath. This was it.

"Good," Vivian said. "The sooner we get this over with, the better."

"Vivian, please," Nancy begged as Dave headed down the stairs with the crate. *"Please . . ."*

"Save it for the guy at the pearly gates." Vivian waved her gun menacingly.

"I guess this is goodbye," George managed to choke out. Nancy had never seen steely-nerved George shed a tear. She dropped her head, expecting the gunshot. But instead, she heard an ear-shattering scream!

Chapter Fifteen

NANCY JERKED HER head up to see Vivian drenched in a steaming liquid. And wrestling the gun from her hand was . . .

"Alan!" Nancy cried out. "How on earth?"

Alan stood behind Vivian, holding her gun in one hand and a huge bowl in the other. "Hot egg drop soup," he grinned. Working swiftly, he untied his friends. "I figured the last place those muscle-brains would look for me was in their own building. I sneaked back in through the restaurant side and came up the dumbwaiter. You were right, Nancy. It was *not* the most comfortable ride." Alan unknotted the last bonds.

"Alan," Nancy said gratefully, "without you, we'd—"

"—never have gotten into this mess in the first place. The least I could do was save your skin."

Before Nancy could reply, footsteps on the stairs signaled Dave's return. "Okay, guys," she whispered. "You're going to have to take Li's henchmen on your own. I'm afraid my shoulder's given out on me."

"I thought you said it was fine," George scolded her.

"So I lied. I don't think I'm up for any fancy karate moves."

"It's all right, Nancy," said Roger Gold. "Even without you, it's nine of us against four of them."

Suddenly, Dave appeared in the room along with Li's other bullies. "Hey, what's going on? Viv, what are you doing on the fl—"

Dave caught a right to his jaw before the word was out of his mouth. The small room reverberated with sounds of punches, kicks, and heated exclamations.

It didn't take long for Nancy's friends to overpower Li's cohorts. "Good job," Nancy said breathlessly. "Alan, go down and see about those policemen. Take Vivian's gun, just in case."

Alan left the room and a few seconds later reappeared with four men in blue uniforms.

"Sergeant Wald," Nancy said, pointing to Dave, Vivian, and the other three men, "we have a little present for you. But there's one more. The boss, James Li. He's trying to escape on a ship that's about to pull anchor. Li told his boys he'd leave without the merchandise if he had to. Do you think we can stop him?"

"That should be easy." Sergeant Wald stepped forward. "Just tell us what dock he's leaving from, and we can radio headquarters. They'll have cars and a special navy unit over there in no time."

Nancy turned toward Li's little gang, now securely tied with the ropes that had held her and her friends just moments earlier. "Okay, which one of you wants to tell me where your boss is leaving from?"

Dave and the others remained silent.

"Do you think he'd do the same for you?" Nancy asked. "No way. He wouldn't stick his neck out one fraction of an inch. In fact, he's getting ready to leave without you right this second."

No answer.

"Dave, think about what James Li left you to do. He didn't want to do it himself, so who did he stick with it?"

Dave scowled. "Yeah, that bum."

"Come on, tell us," Nancy urged. She'd learned in karate class that a chain was most easily broken at its weakest link. "Maybe if you cooperate, they'll let you off with a lighter sentence."

"Don't listen to her," Vivian commanded.

Dave looked from his girlfriend to Nancy, and back to his girlfriend.

"You know, your mother would be heartbroken to see her son locked away forever," Nancy said, trying a different tack.

"How do you know what my mother would think?" Dave shouted.

"Ned had a little chat with her," Nancy replied calmly. "We were trying to track you down."

Dave's face went from furious to panicked. The chain snapped. "All right, you win. I'll tell you where he is."

Nancy allowed herself a long overdue sigh of relief.

She was safe. Bess and Barton were fine. And Li's gang was about to be put away. It was true that her shoulder ached, that her wrists and ankles were sore where Dave had tied them, and that her head was still bruised from where he had hit her the first night. But she had never in her life felt happier or more alive!

That happy feeling was still with Nancy the next morning as she flounced down on the edge of Bess's bed. She steadied herself with her left arm, since her right one was still sore from the previous night. "Come on, lazybones! Do you want to sleep through your last day in New York?"

Bess groaned and pulled the covers over her head.

"Bess!" Nancy jostled her friend's leg through the blanket. "It's almost eleven o'clock."

Bess peeked one half-open eye out from her cocoon. "Nan, don't you know that people who've been through traumas need lots of rest?" She rolled over on her stomach.

"You seemed just fine at our midnight celebration supper. Remember putting away all those spare ribs?"

George came out of the bathroom, a towel wrapped like a turban around her wet hair. "Don't even mention spare ribs. I ate enough last night for the rest of the week."

"And you're going to eat even more this afternoon at that luncheon the Chinatown Neighborhood Association is giving for us," Nancy reminded her. "Mrs. Chen, she's president of the association, told me that the community is incredibly grateful to all of us for helping to put James Li behind bars. What a bully! It wasn't enough for him to pirate records and run all those other big-time illegal operations the police told us he had going. No, he had to muscle in on the small businesses in Chinatown, too."

"Yeah, I can certainly understand why the community is so glad to see him go," George said. "And it's really nice of them to give us an honorary luncheon. But I don't know if I'm going to be able to touch it." She patted her lean, flat stomach.

"Don't worry. I'll help you out." Bess finally

sat up in bed and stretched her arms over her head.

George rolled her eyes. "Well, look who finally rises at the mention of her favorite sport—eating."

"Oh, come on, give me a break. How often do you get some of the best Chinese chefs this side of the Pacific to make a special meal just for you?"

"Not too often," George answered. "And speaking of not too often, there's something I've been wanting to ask you, Bess."

"Yeah?"

"Alan said he went down to World Communications yesterday while you were out jogging. Since when have you turned into a jock?"

Bess made a face. "We-e-ell . . . I sort of ended up doing more shopping than jogging . . ."

"Figures," George said. "So how much did that little jog cost you?"

Bess cringed. "I don't think I should say."

"Come on, spill it. What'd you blow?"

Bess pouted. "George, don't tell me you've never gone out on a spur-of-the-moment shopping spree. How about that time you bought all those weights from the sports shop to use at home, and then you joined the gym, so you don't even *need* your own weights?"

George frowned. "Well, at least I don't go out running with a shopping bag and my wallet."

Nancy sighed. "Okay, you two. No more arguing. From now on, this vacation's going to be fun, fun, fun."

"Famous last words," George said.

Nancy shot George a mock glare. "Don't even think it," she said. "It *is* going to be a vacation. Even if it's for just one more day."

"Yeah, I wouldn't mind some fun today either," Bess agreed. "I think I deserve it after yesterday. Now I know where the expression 'scared to death' comes from. I honestly believed I was going to die of fright before those thugs even did anything to me."

Nancy leaned over and tugged on Bess's blond hair. "I know. It was a nightmare. But it's all over."

"Is it?" Bess punched her pillow, her expression sober. "Maybe for you, but I've got some serious thinking to do."

"Alan?" Nancy asked softly.

Bess nodded. "He told lies to get what he wanted. I didn't realize the boy I fell in love with would do something like that."

George pulled a chair up next to the bed. "But he also saved our lives. Bess, your boyfriend's a hero."

"Maybe."

"Barton and Roger sure seem to think so," Nancy put in. "They wouldn't have offered to help him out otherwise."

"Yeah, just think of it, Bess. He might get his dream one day, after all," George remarked.

"I'm thinking of it. But I'm also thinking that I want to take it more slowly with him. What happened made me realize that there's a lot about Alan Wales I don't know."

"But you still feel something for him, don't you?" Nancy asked.

"Well, when the chemistry's right . . ." Bess's round face grew pink.

"Good. Because I told Mrs. Chen to seat you two next to each other," Nancy said with a laugh. "Oh, did I tell you that my dad's bringing Ann Nordquist to the luncheon?"

George's brown eyes opened wide. "Talk about chemistry!"

"Yeah. Dad's really enjoying her company." Nancy sighed. "I can't tell you how glad I am to have a suspect turn out innocent."

"And speaking of couples," George said, giving Nancy a poke, "how are you and Ned doing?"

"I think we're going to be all right." Nancy smiled brightly. "As a matter of fact, this afternoon he's taking me on a very special boat ride to a tiny island!" She raised her eyebrows suggestively. "It's a start."

"Sounds romantic," Bess sighed.

Nancy giggled. "Yeah, it's called the ferry to the Statue of Liberty! Now how about getting up,

Bess, or the guests of honor are going to miss their own luncheon."

"And don't take too long putting on your makeup," George added.

"Okay, okay." Bess climbed out of bed. "Are Barton and Roger and all the Fenders going to be there?"

"Absolutely," Nancy replied. "Hey, did you know that Barton told me he's going to write a song about us and the whole mystery? He's going to call it 'Scared to Death.'"

"Wow! You mean every time we turn on our radios in River Heights we're going to hear about ourselves?" Bess asked.

"An instant souvenir," Nancy answered.

"Maybe they'll even make it into a video," George said hopefully.

"That would be neat," Nancy agreed. "And I know just the threesome to play the detective and her two friends. . . ."